BATMAN
THE BRAVE AND THE BOLD®

STONE ARCH BOOKS
a capstone imprint

STONE ARCH BOOKS™
Published in 2012
A Capstone Imprint
1710 Roe Crest Drive
North Mankato, MN 56003
www.capstonepub.com

Originally published by DC Comics in
the U.S. in single magazine form as
Batman: The Brave and the Bold #3.

DC Comics
1700 Broadway, New York, NY 10019
A Warner Bros. Entertainment Company

Cataloging-in-Publication Data is available at the
Library of Congress website:
ISBN: 978-1-4342-4547-2 (library binding)

Summary: When the Ultra-Humanite wants to score big, he goes straight to the top - he's after the President! But Batman and Green Arrow have a daring rescue plan.

STONE ARCH BOOKS
Ashley C. Andersen Zantop *Publisher*
Michael Dahl *Editorial Director*
Donald Lemke & Christianne Jones *Editors*
Heather Kindseth *Creative Director*
Hilary Wacholz *Designer*
Kathy McColley *Production Specialist*

DC COMICS
Rachel Gluckstern & Michael Siglain *Original U.S. Editors*
Harvey Richards *U.S. Assistant Editor*
James Tucker *Cover Artist*

Printed in the United States of America
in Brainer, Minnesota.
122012 007078R

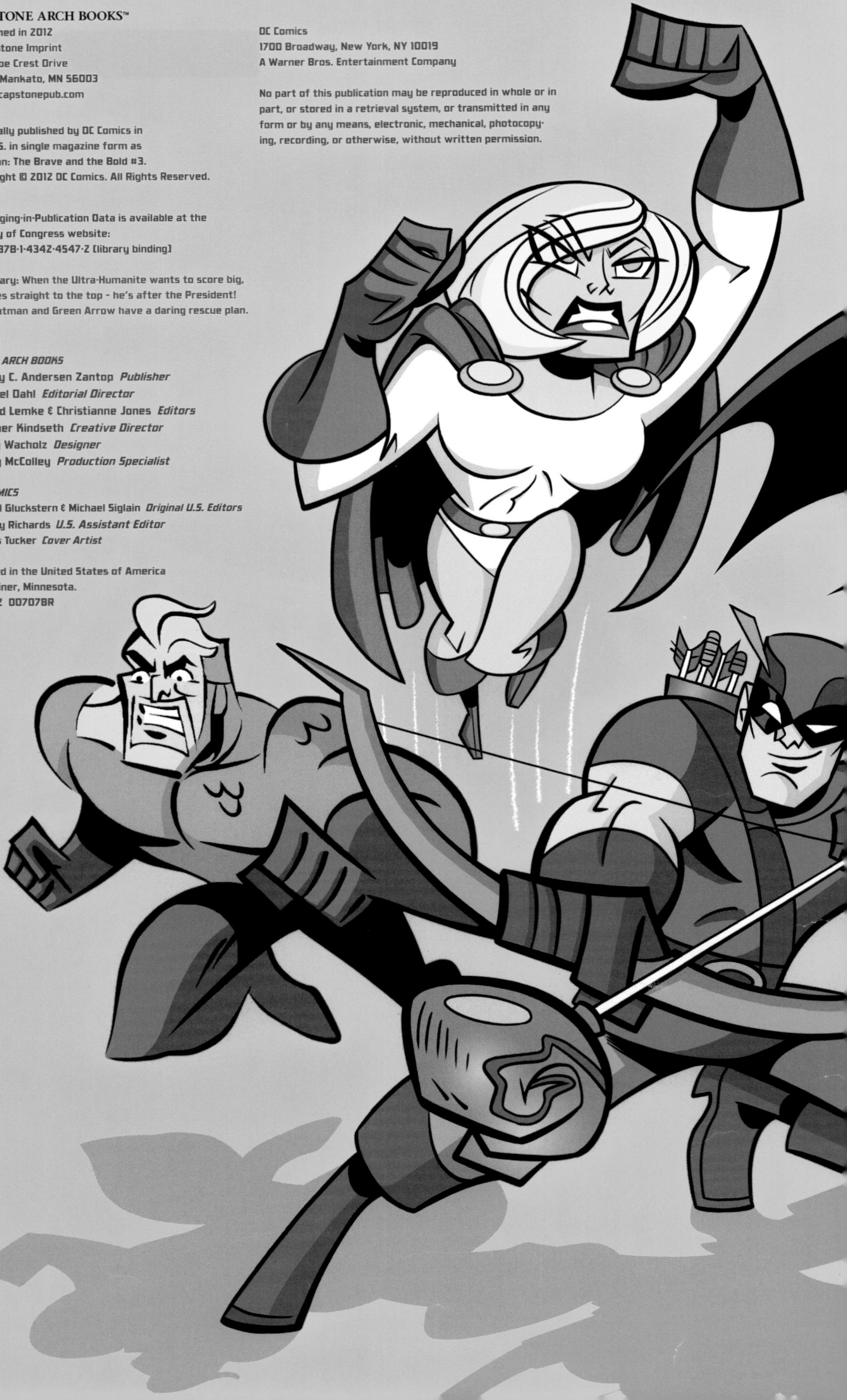

BATMAN
THE BRAVE AND THE BOLD®

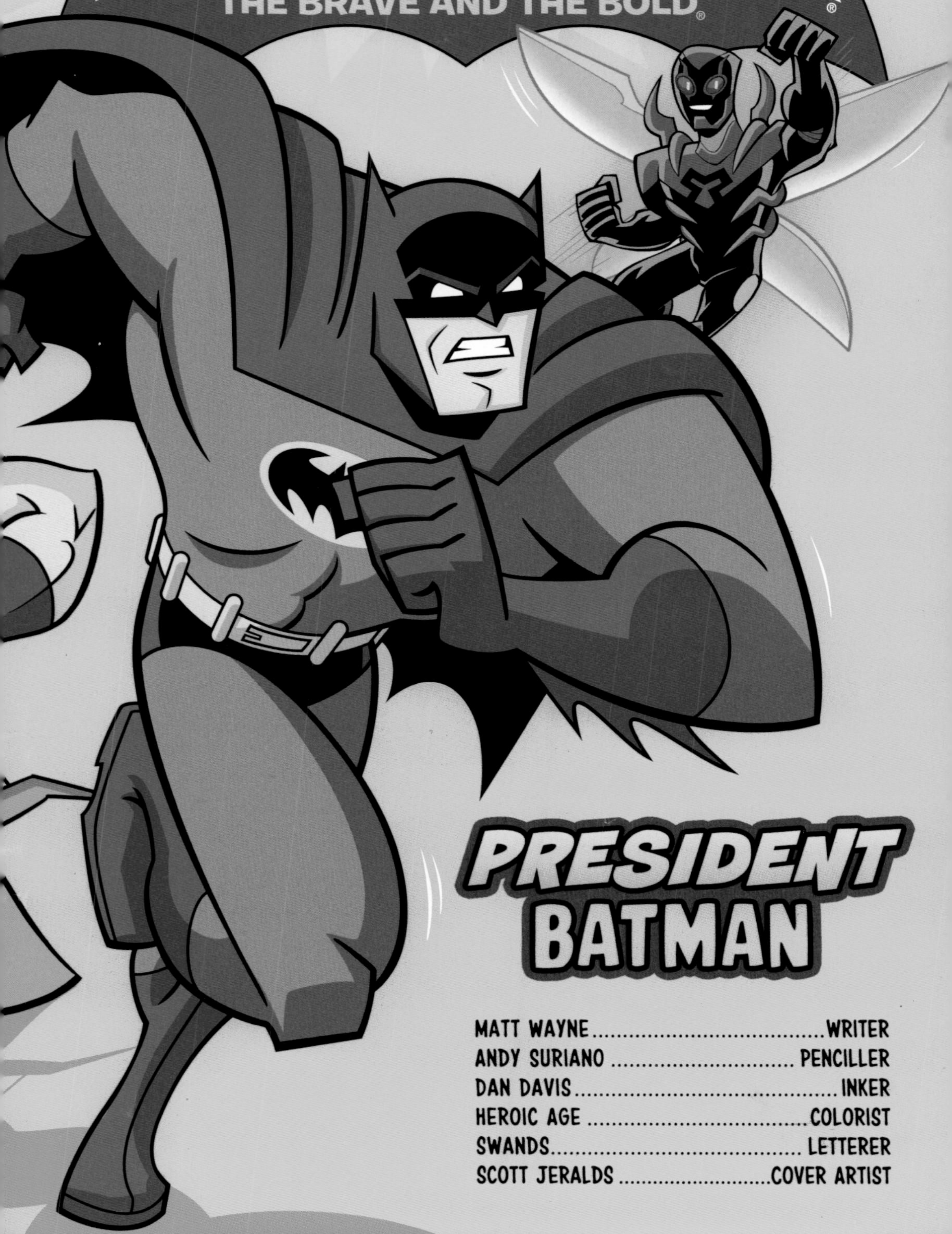

PRESIDENT BATMAN

MATT WAYNE....................................WRITER
ANDY SURIANO .... PENCILLER
DAN DAVIS..INKER
HEROIC AGE ....COLORIST
SWANDS... LETTERER
SCOTT JERALDS ....COVER ARTIST

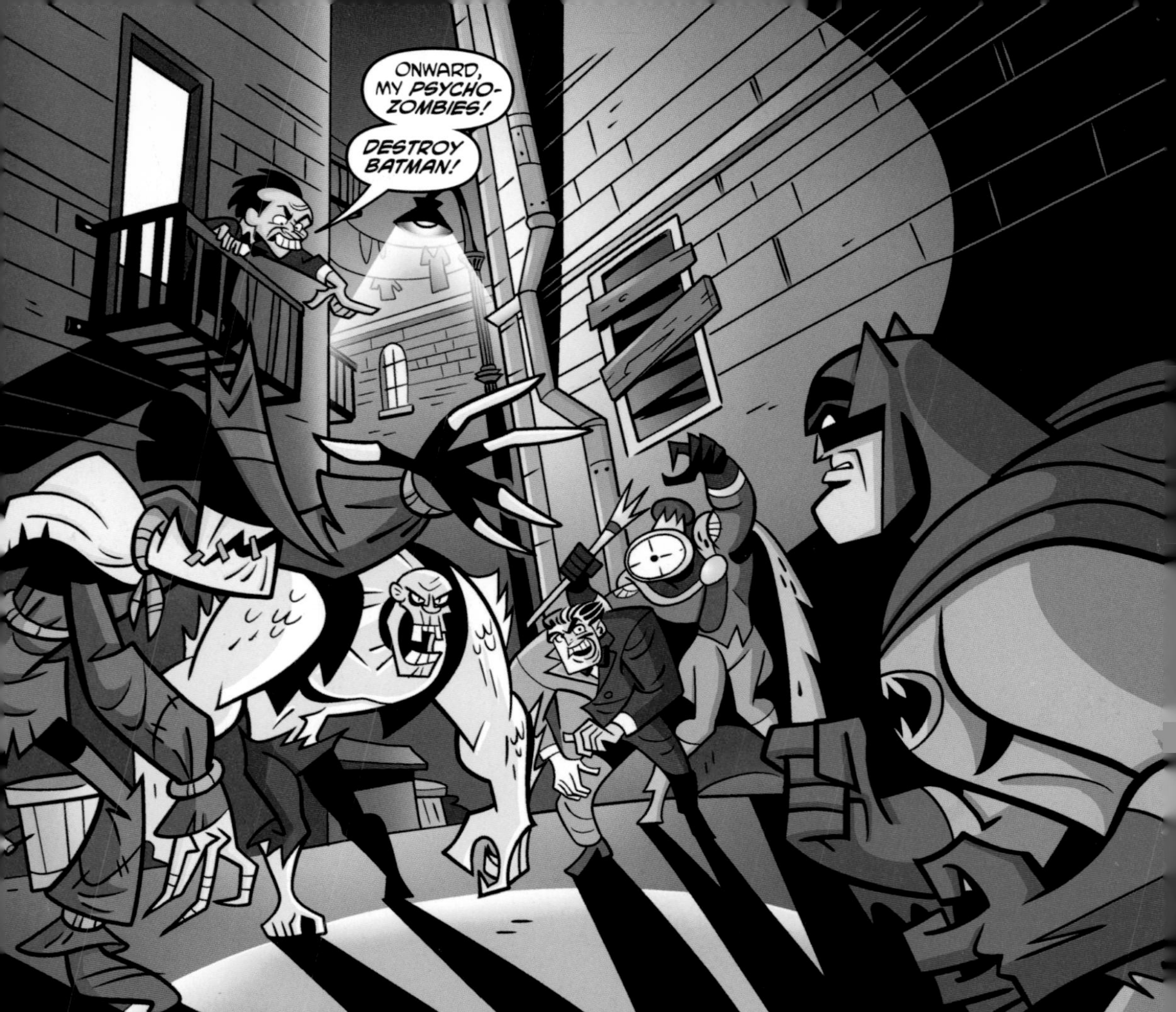
ONWARD, MY PSYCHO-ZOMBIES!
DESTROY BATMAN!

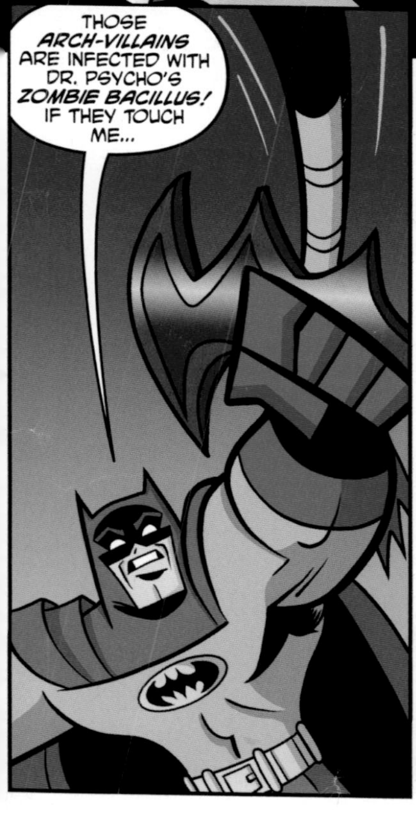
THOSE ARCH-VILLAINS ARE INFECTED WITH DR. PSYCHO'S ZOMBIE BACILLUS! IF THEY TOUCH ME...

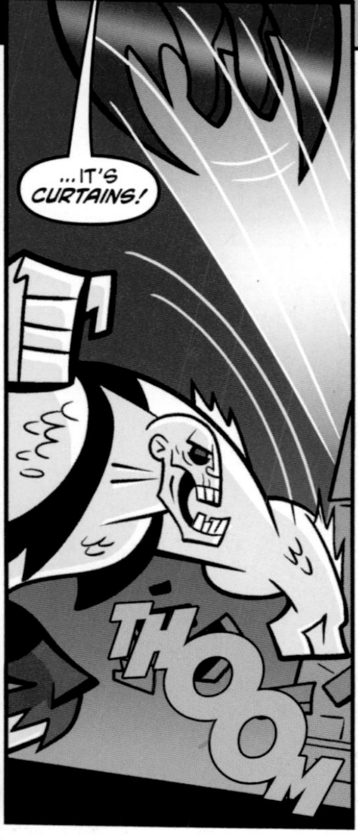
...IT'S CURTAINS!
THOOOM

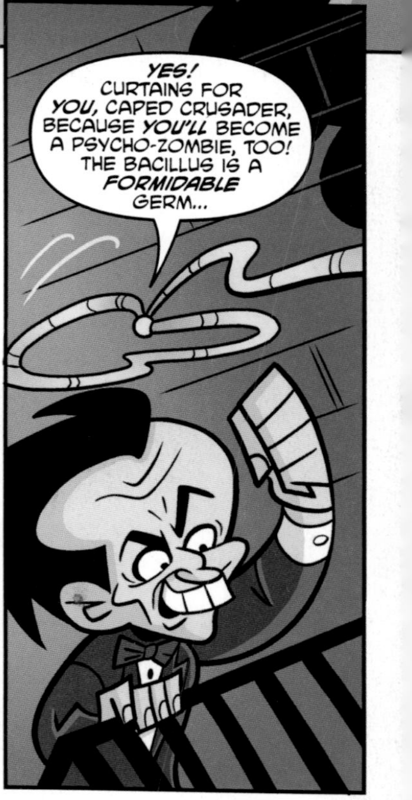
YES! CURTAINS FOR YOU, CAPED CRUSADER, BECAUSE YOU'LL BECOME A PSYCHO-ZOMBIE, TOO! THE BACILLUS IS A FORMIDABLE GERM...

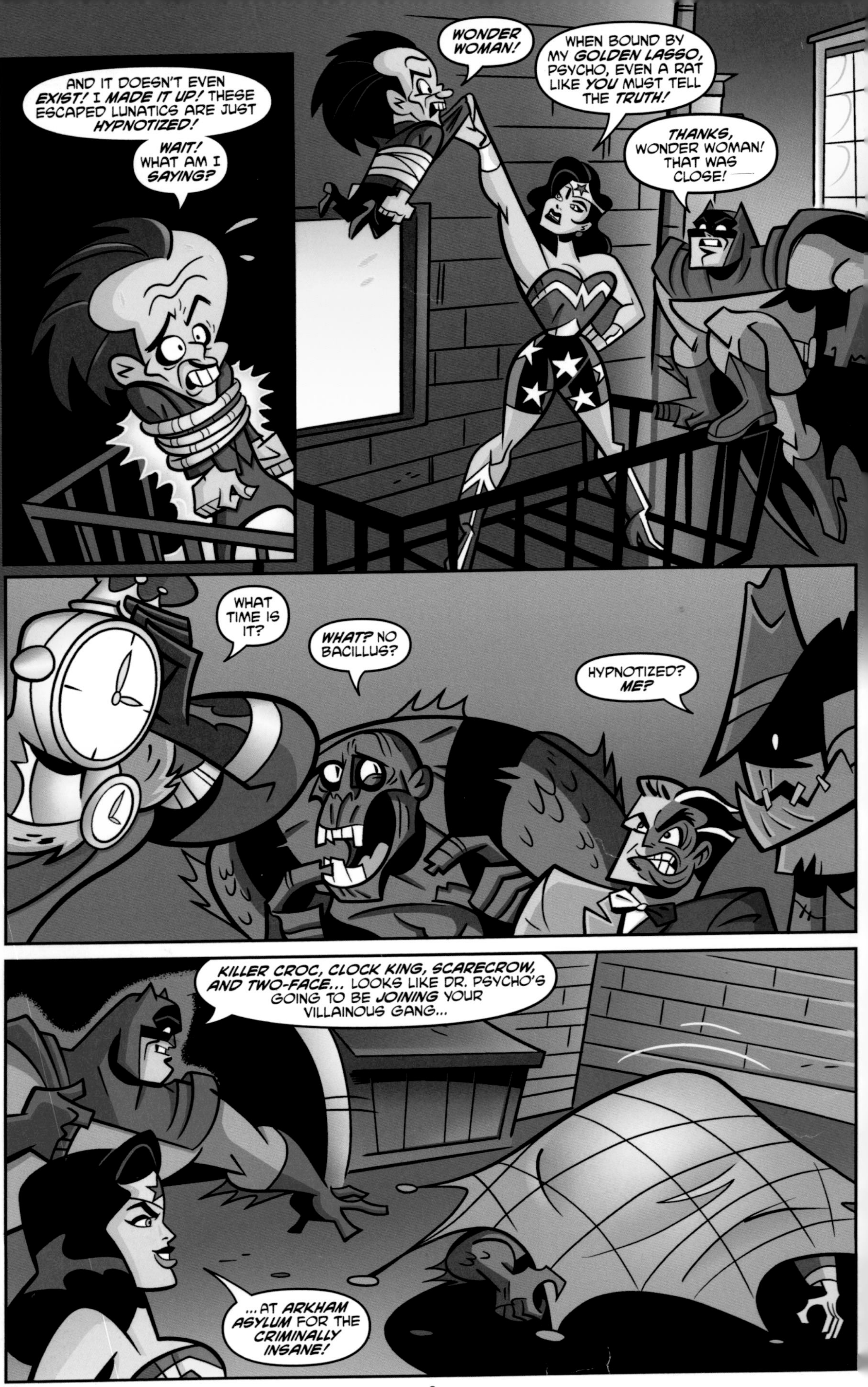
AND IT DOESN'T EVEN EXIST! I MADE IT UP! THESE ESCAPED LUNATICS ARE JUST HYPNOTIZED!
WAIT! WHAT AM I SAYING?
WONDER WOMAN!
WHEN BOUND BY MY GOLDEN LASSO, PSYCHO, EVEN A RAT LIKE YOU MUST TELL THE TRUTH!
THANKS, WONDER WOMAN! THAT WAS CLOSE!
WHAT TIME IS IT?
WHAT? NO BACILLUS?
HYPNOTIZED? ME?
KILLER CROC, CLOCK KING, SCARECROW, AND TWO-FACE... LOOKS LIKE DR. PSYCHO'S GOING TO BE JOINING YOUR VILLAINOUS GANG...
...AT ARKHAM ASYLUM FOR THE CRIMINALLY INSANE!

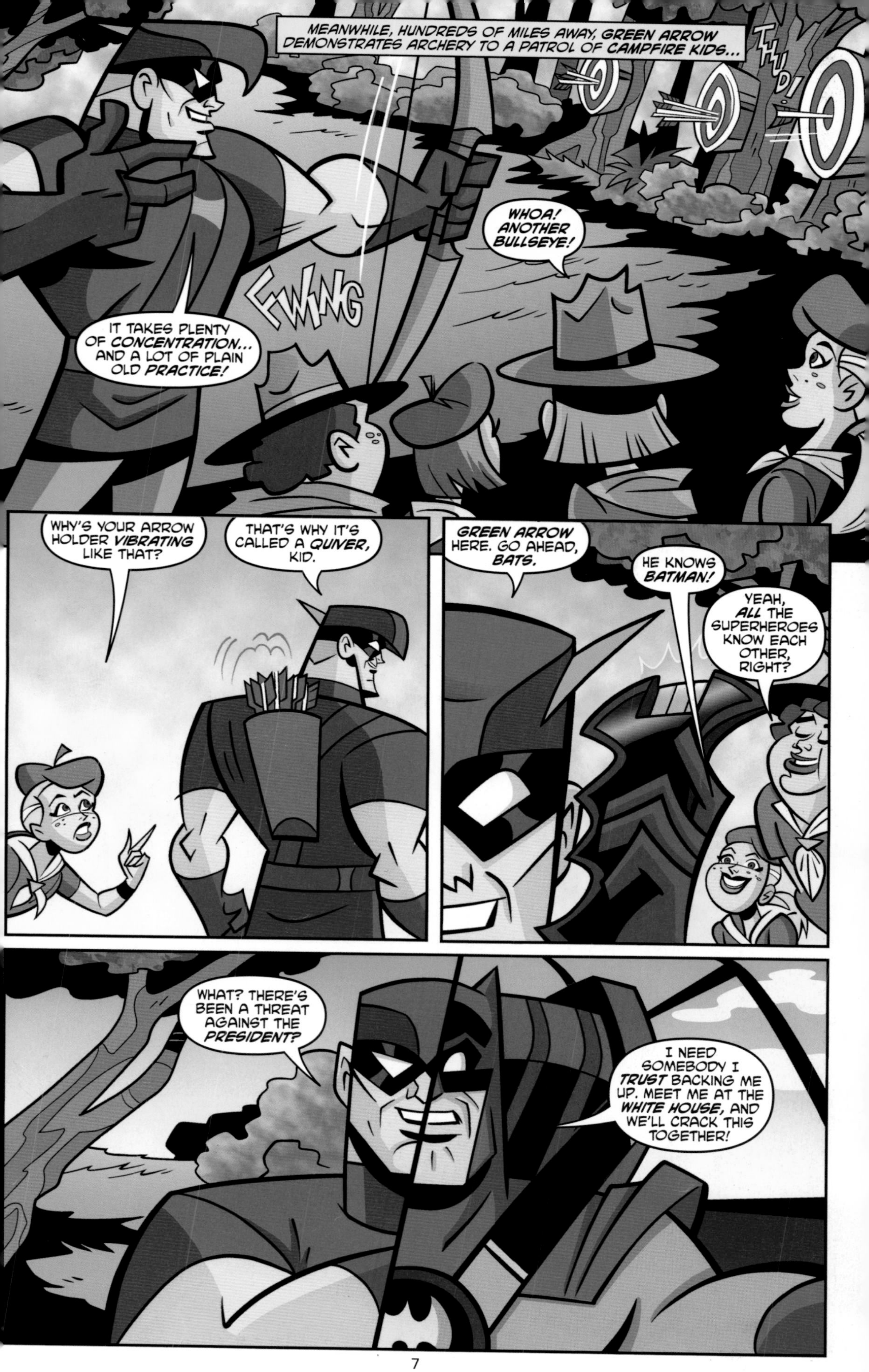
MEANWHILE, HUNDREDS OF MILES AWAY, GREEN ARROW DEMONSTRATES ARCHERY TO A PATROL OF CAMPFIRE KIDS...
THUD!
FWING
WHOA! ANOTHER BULLSEYE!
IT TAKES PLENTY OF CONCENTRATION... AND A LOT OF PLAIN OLD PRACTICE!
WHY'S YOUR ARROW HOLDER VIBRATING LIKE THAT?
THAT'S WHY IT'S CALLED A QUIVER, KID.
GREEN ARROW HERE. GO AHEAD, BATS.
HE KNOWS BATMAN!
YEAH, ALL THE SUPERHEROES KNOW EACH OTHER, RIGHT?
WHAT? THERE'S BEEN A THREAT AGAINST THE PRESIDENT?
I NEED SOMEBODY I TRUST BACKING ME UP. MEET ME AT THE WHITE HOUSE, AND WE'LL CRACK THIS TOGETHER!

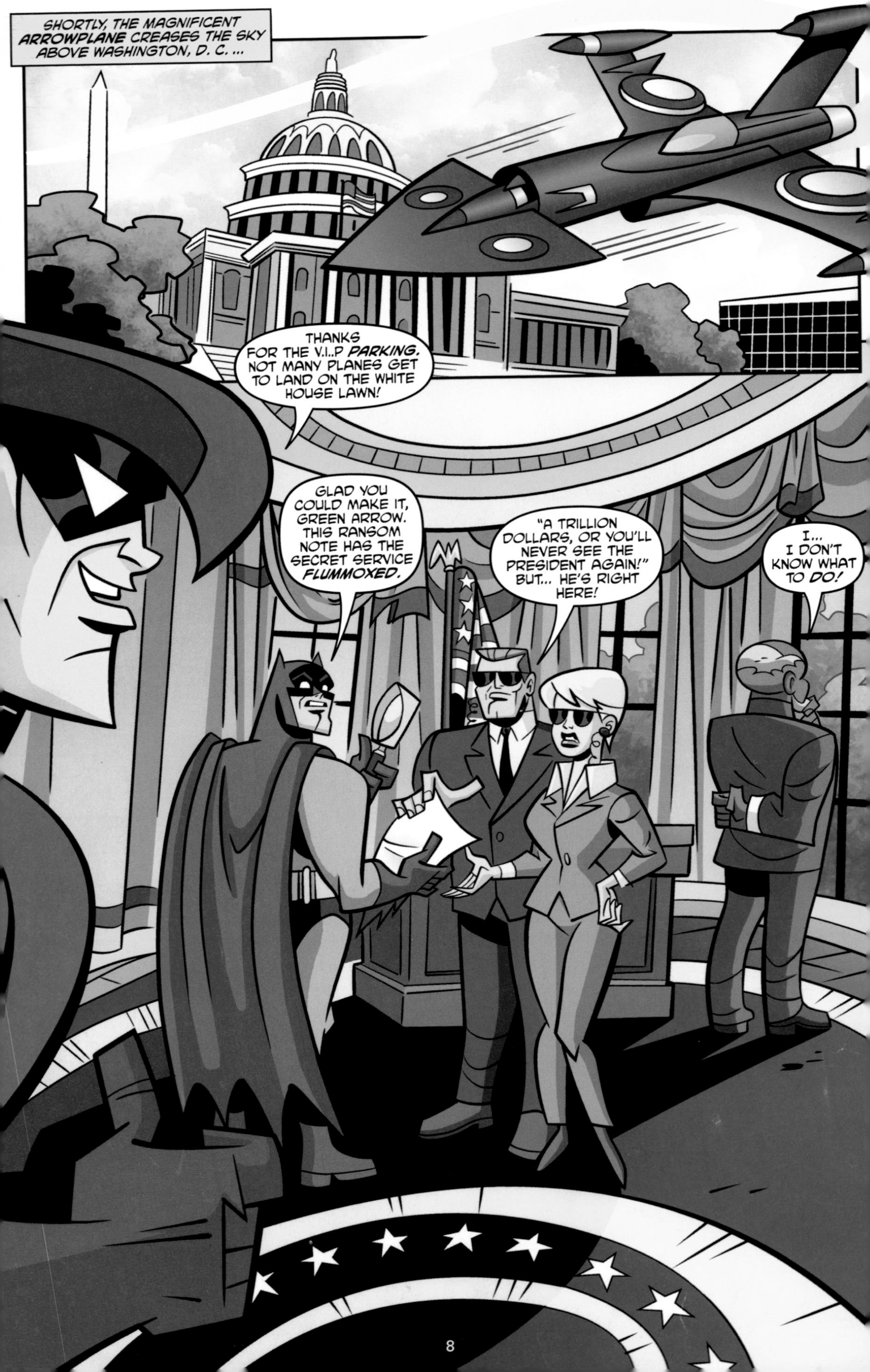

SHORTLY, THE MAGNIFICENT ARROWPLANE CREASES THE SKY ABOVE WASHINGTON, D. C. ...
THANKS FOR THE V.I..P PARKING. NOT MANY PLANES GET TO LAND ON THE WHITE HOUSE LAWN!
GLAD YOU COULD MAKE IT, GREEN ARROW. THIS RANSOM NOTE HAS THE SECRET SERVICE FLUMMOXED.
"A TRILLION DOLLARS, OR YOU'LL NEVER SEE THE PRESIDENT AGAIN!" BUT... HE'S RIGHT HERE!
I... I DON'T KNOW WHAT TO DO!

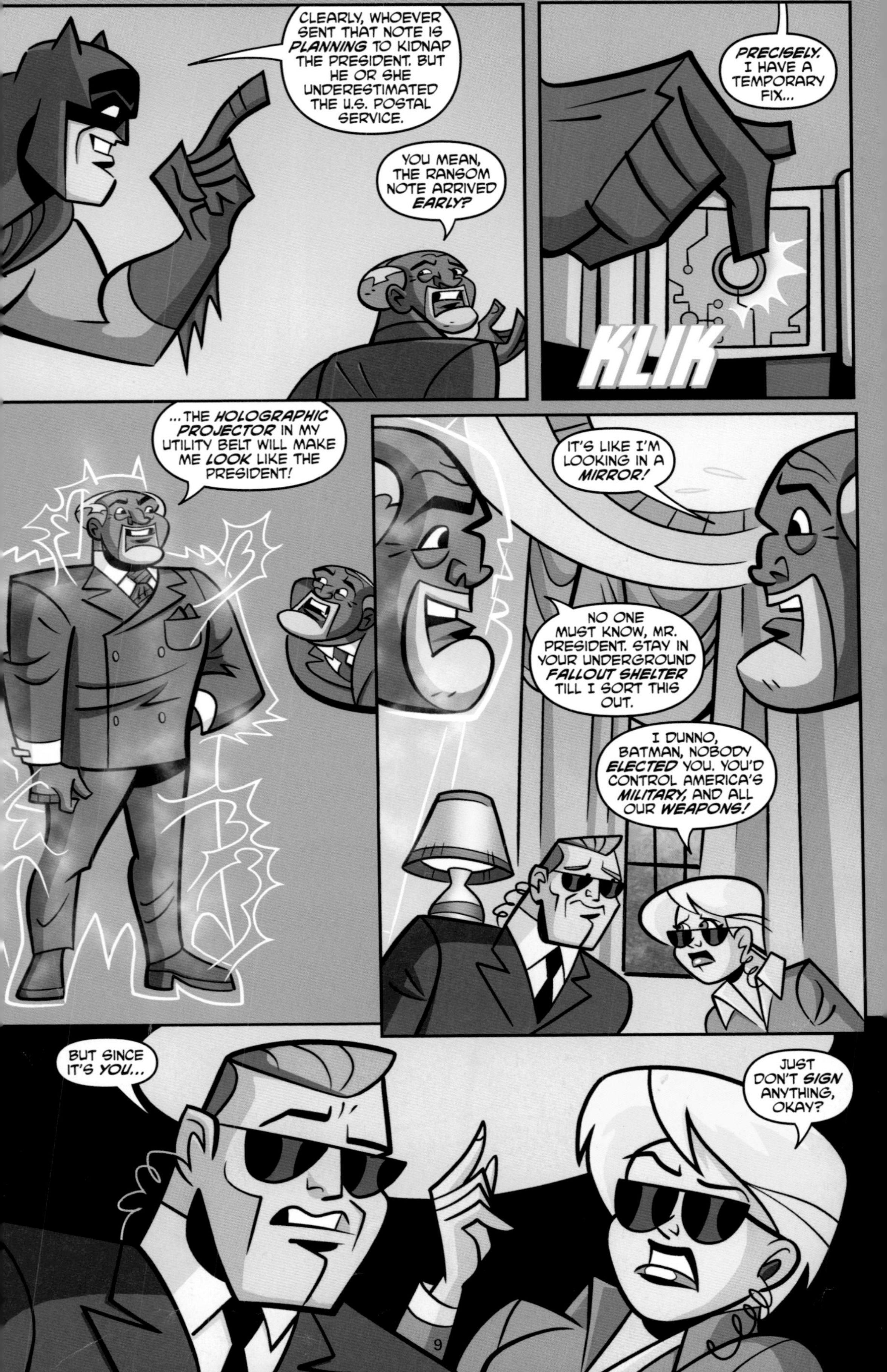
CLEARLY, WHOEVER SENT THAT NOTE IS *PLANNING* TO KIDNAP THE PRESIDENT. BUT HE OR SHE UNDERESTIMATED THE U.S. POSTAL SERVICE.
YOU MEAN, THE RANSOM NOTE ARRIVED *EARLY?*
PRECISELY. I HAVE A TEMPORARY FIX...
KLIK
...THE *HOLOGRAPHIC PROJECTOR* IN MY UTILITY BELT WILL MAKE ME *LOOK* LIKE THE PRESIDENT!
IT'S LIKE I'M LOOKING IN A *MIRROR!*
NO ONE MUST KNOW, MR. PRESIDENT. STAY IN YOUR UNDERGROUND *FALLOUT SHELTER* TILL I SORT THIS OUT.
I DUNNO, BATMAN, NOBODY *ELECTED* YOU. YOU'D CONTROL AMERICA'S *MILITARY,* AND ALL OUR *WEAPONS!*
BUT SINCE IT'S *YOU...*
JUST DON'T *SIGN* ANYTHING, OKAY?

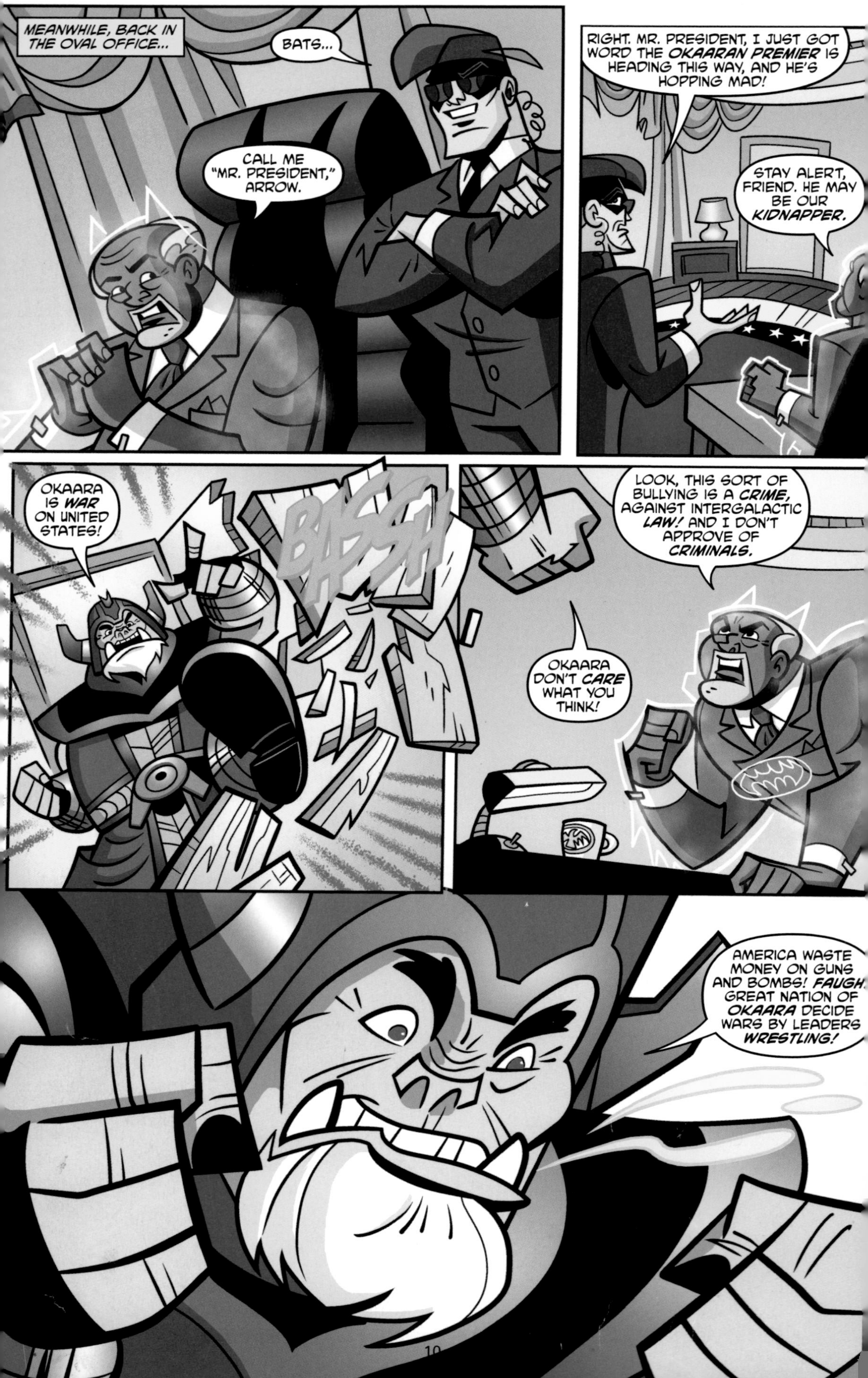
MEANWHILE, BACK IN THE OVAL OFFICE...
BATS...
CALL ME "MR. PRESIDENT," ARROW.
RIGHT. MR. PRESIDENT, I JUST GOT WORD THE OKAARAN PREMIER IS HEADING THIS WAY, AND HE'S HOPPING MAD!
STAY ALERT, FRIEND. HE MAY BE OUR KIDNAPPER.
BASSH
OKAARA IS WAR ON UNITED STATES!
LOOK, THIS SORT OF BULLYING IS A CRIME, AGAINST INTERGALACTIC LAW! AND I DON'T APPROVE OF CRIMINALS.
OKAARA DON'T CARE WHAT YOU THINK!
AMERICA WASTE MONEY ON GUNS AND BOMBS! FAUGH. GREAT NATION OF OKAARA DECIDE WARS BY LEADERS WRESTLING!

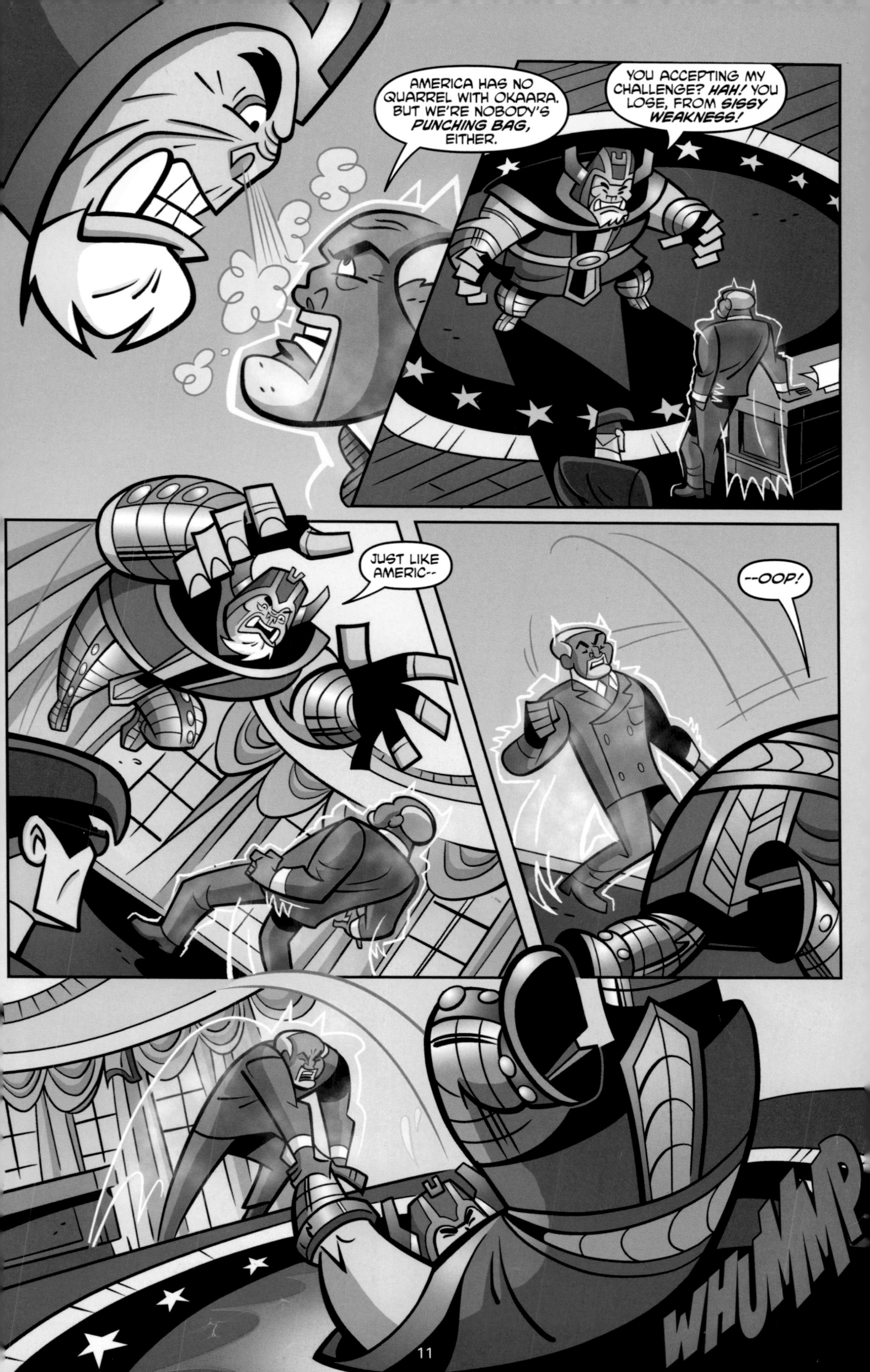
AMERICA HAS NO QUARREL WITH OKAARA. BUT WE'RE NOBODY'S *PUNCHING BAG,* EITHER.
YOU ACCEPTING MY CHALLENGE? *HAH!* YOU LOSE, FROM *SISSY WEAKNESS!*
JUST LIKE AMERIC--
--OOP!
WHUMMP!

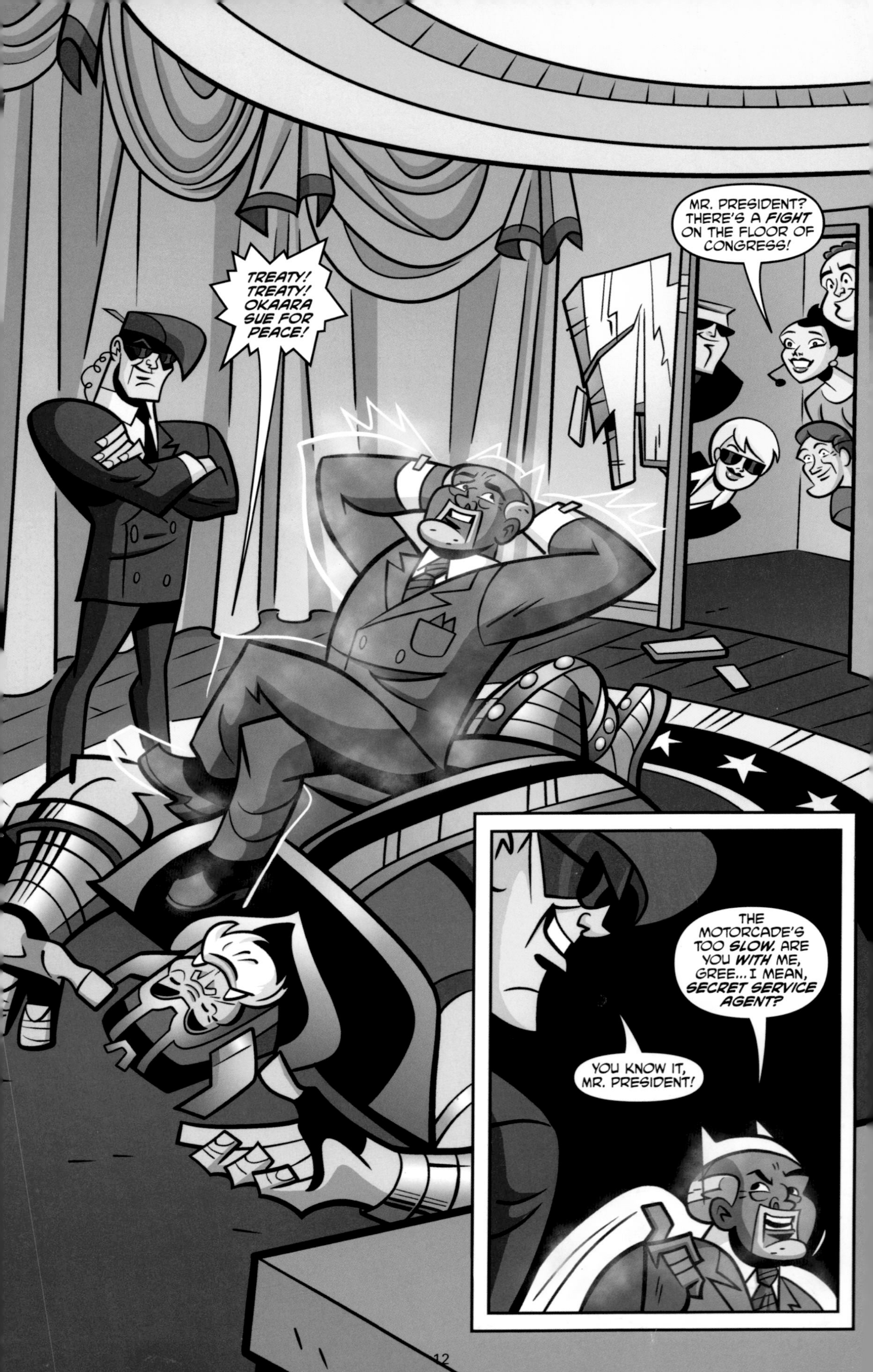
TREATY! TREATY! OKAARA SUE FOR PEACE!
MR. PRESIDENT? THERE'S A FIGHT ON THE FLOOR OF CONGRESS!
THE MOTORCADE'S TOO SLOW. ARE YOU WITH ME, GREE... I MEAN, SECRET SERVICE AGENT?
YOU KNOW IT, MR. PRESIDENT!

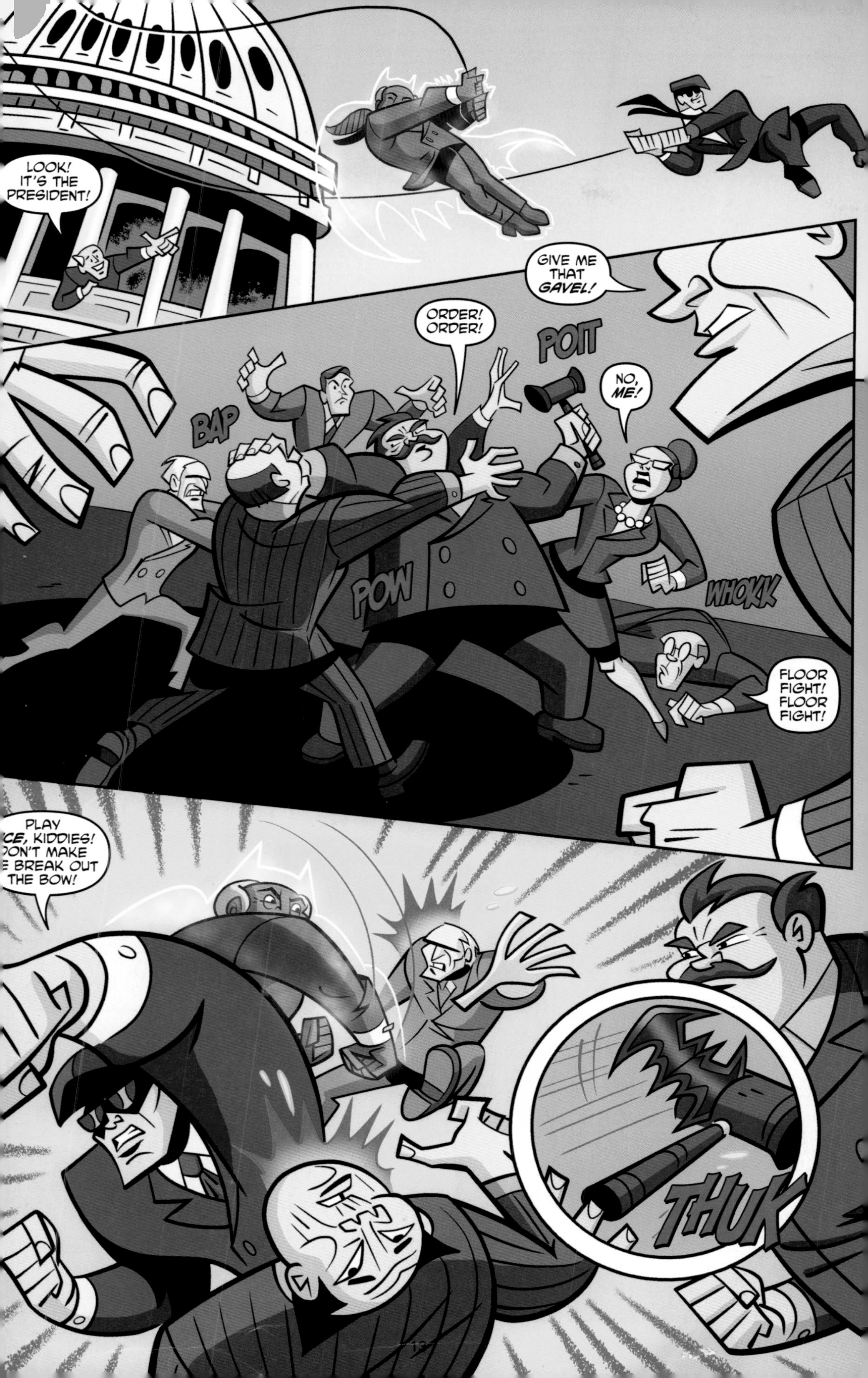
LOOK! IT'S THE PRESIDENT!
GIVE ME THAT *GAVEL!*
ORDER! ORDER!
POIT
NO, *ME!*
BAP
POW
WHOKK
FLOOR FIGHT! FLOOR FIGHT!
PLAY
CE, KIDDIES!
DON'T MAKE
E BREAK OUT
THE BOW!
THUK

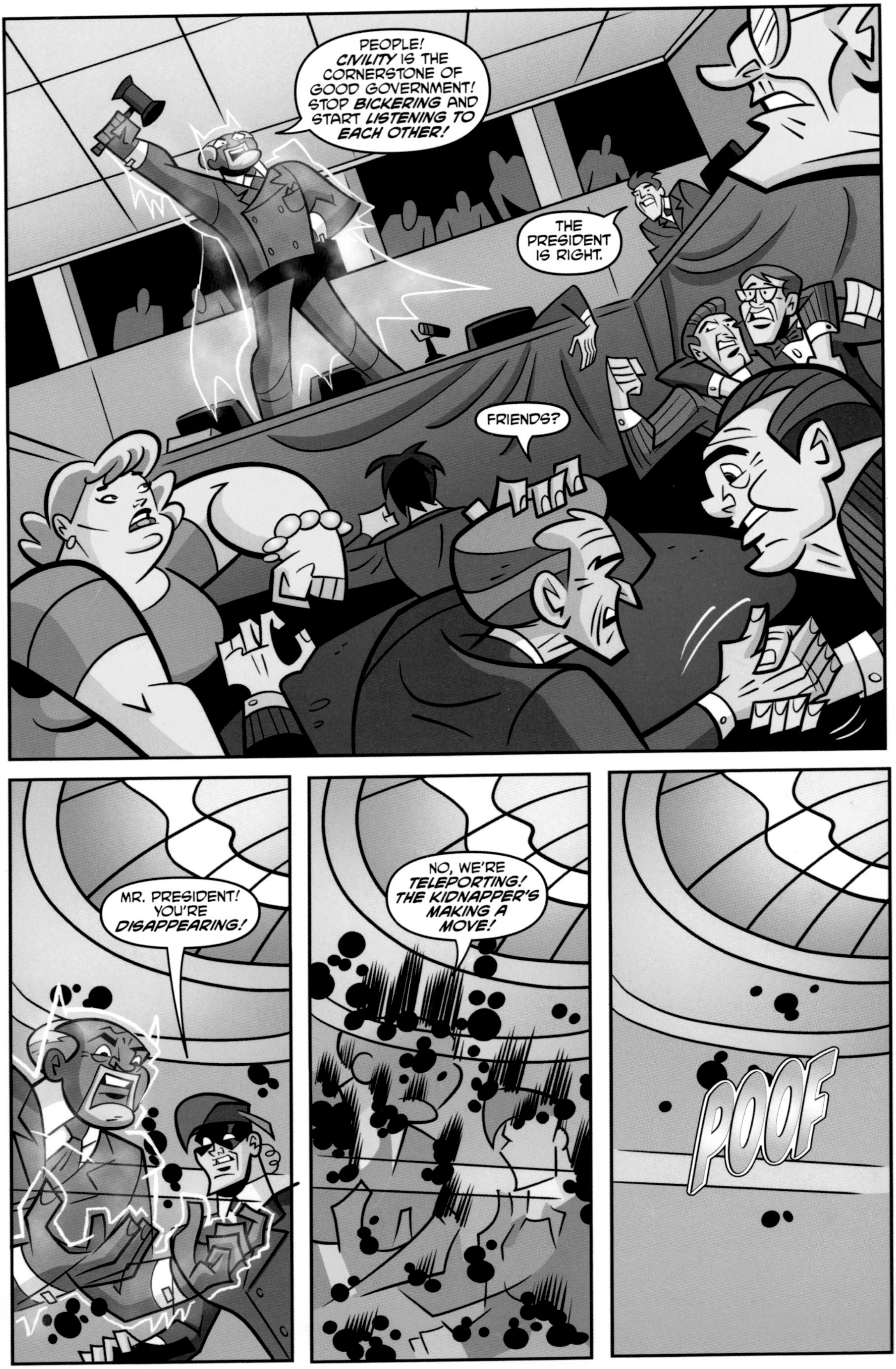
PEOPLE! CIVILITY IS THE CORNERSTONE OF GOOD GOVERNMENT! STOP BICKERING AND START LISTENING TO EACH OTHER!
THE PRESIDENT IS RIGHT.
FRIENDS?
MR. PRESIDENT! YOU'RE DISAPPEARING!
NO, WE'RE TELEPORTING! THE KIDNAPPER'S MAKING A MOVE!
POOF

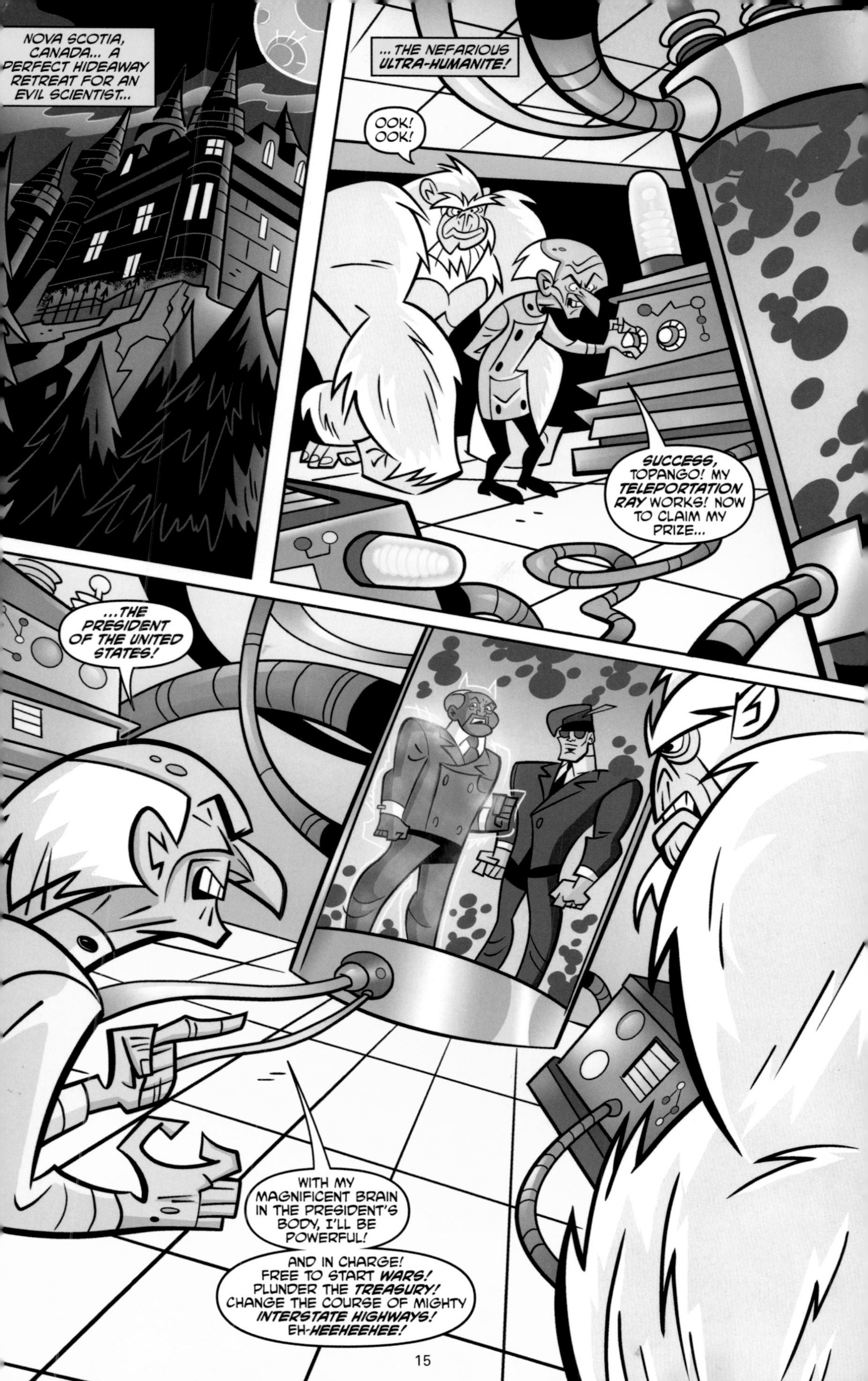
NOVA SCOTIA, CANADA... A PERFECT HIDEAWAY RETREAT FOR AN EVIL SCIENTIST...
...THE NEFARIOUS ULTRA-HUMANITE!
OOK! OOK!
SUCCESS, TOPANGO! MY TELEPORTATION RAY WORKS! NOW TO CLAIM MY PRIZE...
...THE PRESIDENT OF THE UNITED STATES!
WITH MY MAGNIFICENT BRAIN IN THE PRESIDENT'S BODY, I'LL BE POWERFUL!
AND IN CHARGE! FREE TO START WARS! PLUNDER THE TREASURY! CHANGE THE COURSE OF MIGHTY INTERSTATE HIGHWAYS! EH-HEEHEEHEE!

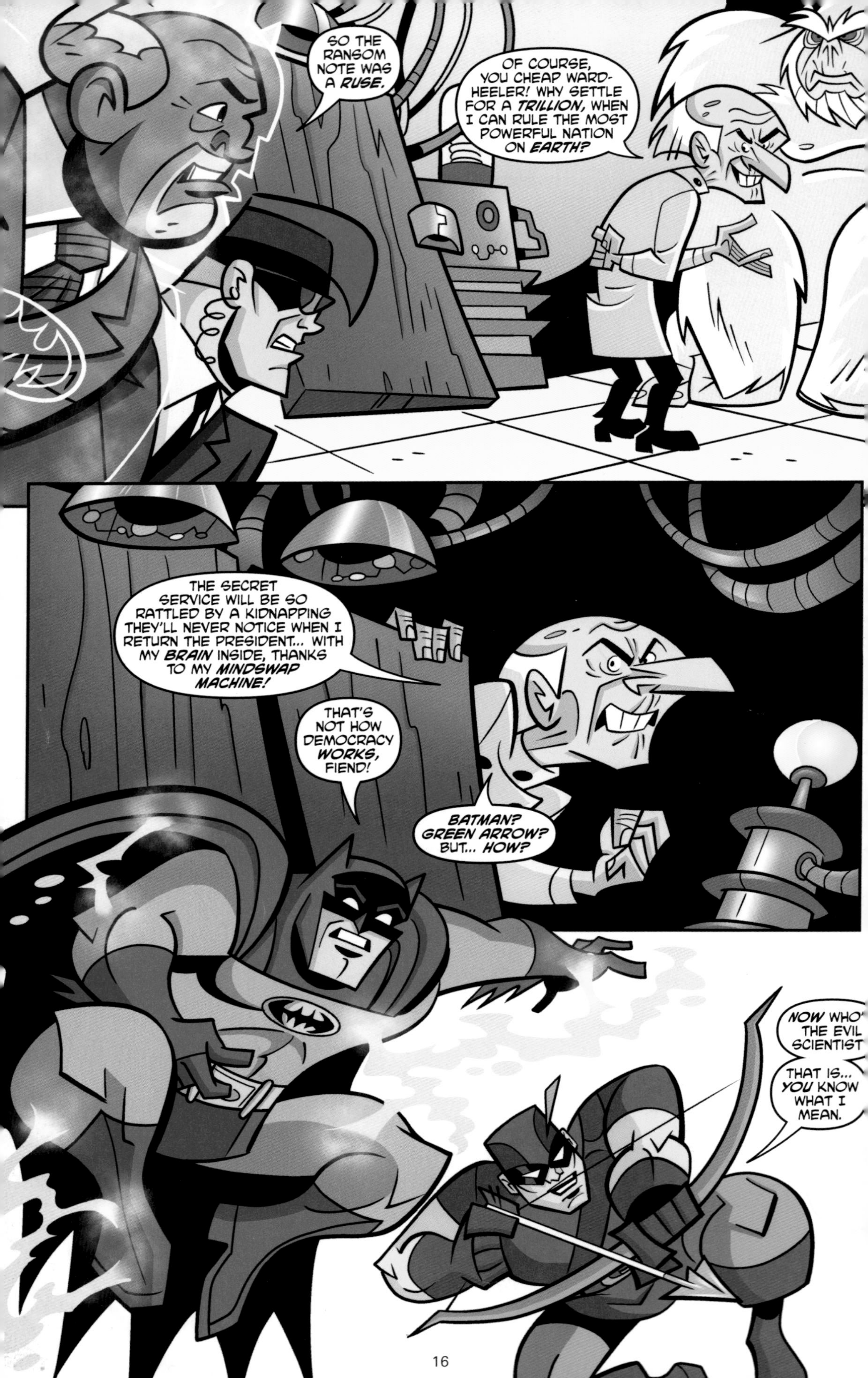
SO THE RANSOM NOTE WAS A *RUSE.*
OF COURSE, YOU CHEAP WARD-HEELER! WHY SETTLE FOR A *TRILLION,* WHEN I CAN RULE THE MOST POWERFUL NATION ON *EARTH?*
THE SECRET SERVICE WILL BE SO RATTLED BY A KIDNAPPING THEY'LL NEVER NOTICE WHEN I RETURN THE PRESIDENT... WITH MY *BRAIN* INSIDE, THANKS TO MY *MINDSWAP MACHINE!*
THAT'S NOT HOW DEMOCRACY *WORKS,* FIEND!
BATMAN? GREEN ARROW? BUT... *HOW?*
NOW WHO' THE EVIL SCIENTIST
THAT IS... *YOU* KNOW WHAT I MEAN.

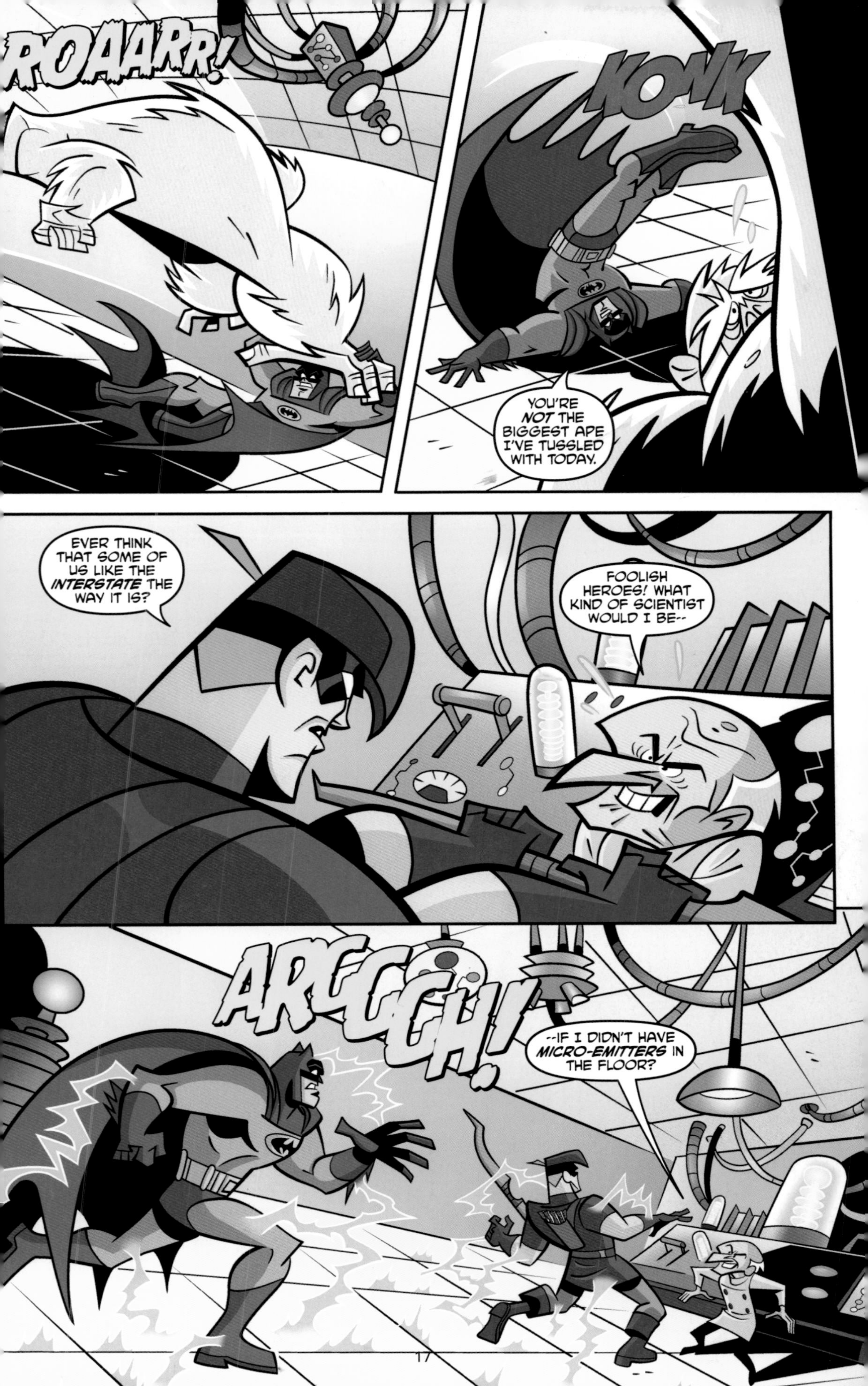
ROAARR!
KONK
YOU'RE NOT THE BIGGEST APE I'VE TUSSLED WITH TODAY.
EVER THINK THAT SOME OF US LIKE THE INTERSTATE THE WAY IT IS?
FOOLISH HEROES! WHAT KIND OF SCIENTIST WOULD I BE--
ARGGGH!
--IF I DIDN'T HAVE MICRO-EMITTERS IN THE FLOOR?

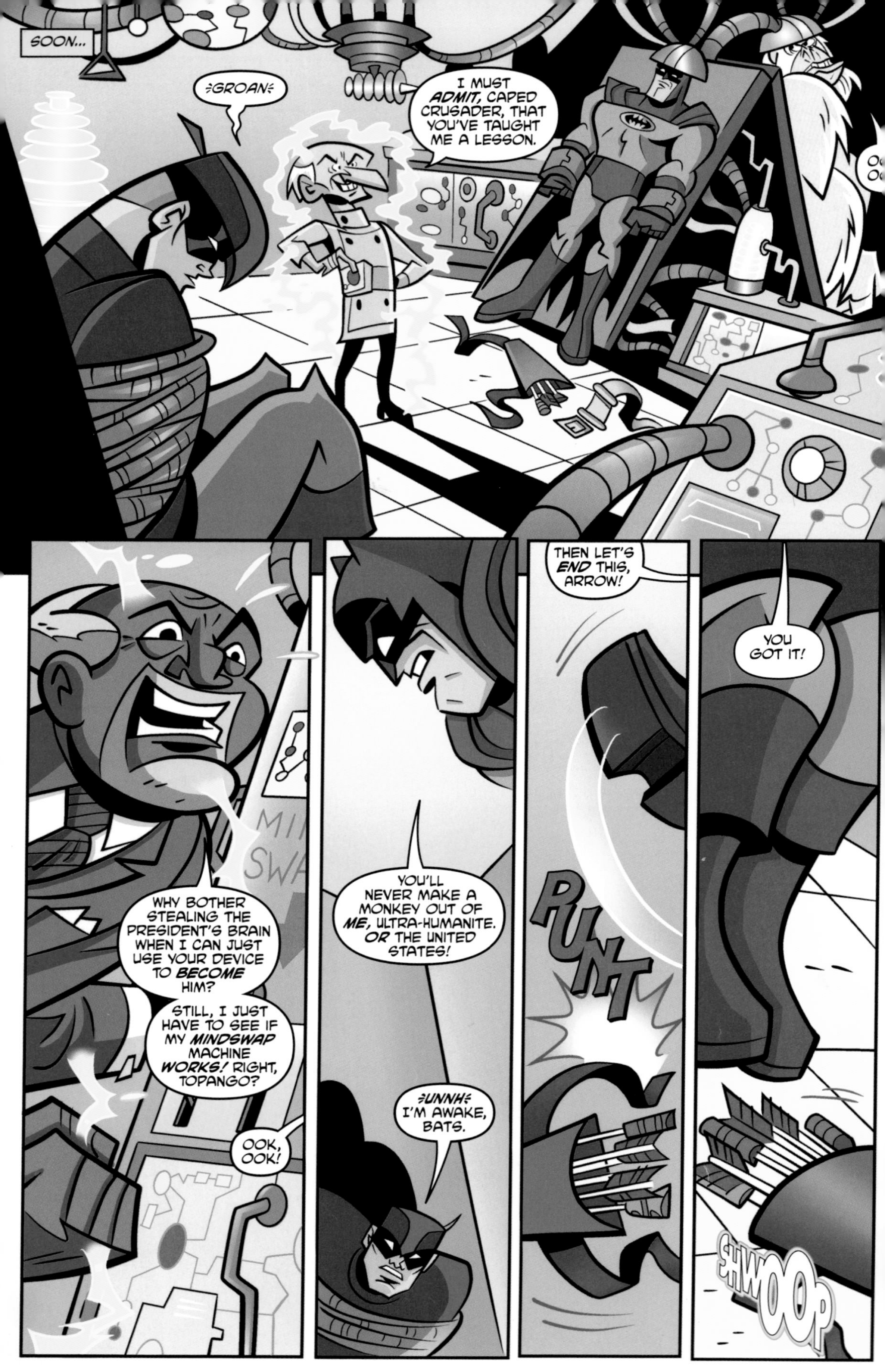
SOON...
GROAN
I MUST ADMIT, CAPED CRUSADER, THAT YOU'VE TAUGHT ME A LESSON.
WHY BOTHER STEALING THE PRESIDENT'S BRAIN WHEN I CAN JUST USE YOUR DEVICE TO BECOME HIM?
STILL, I JUST HAVE TO SEE IF MY MINDSWAP MACHINE WORKS! RIGHT, TOPANGO?
OOK, OOK!
YOU'LL NEVER MAKE A MONKEY OUT OF ME, ULTRA-HUMANITE. OR THE UNITED STATES!
UNNH I'M AWAKE, BATS.
THEN LET'S END THIS, ARROW!
PUNT
YOU GOT IT!
SHWOOP

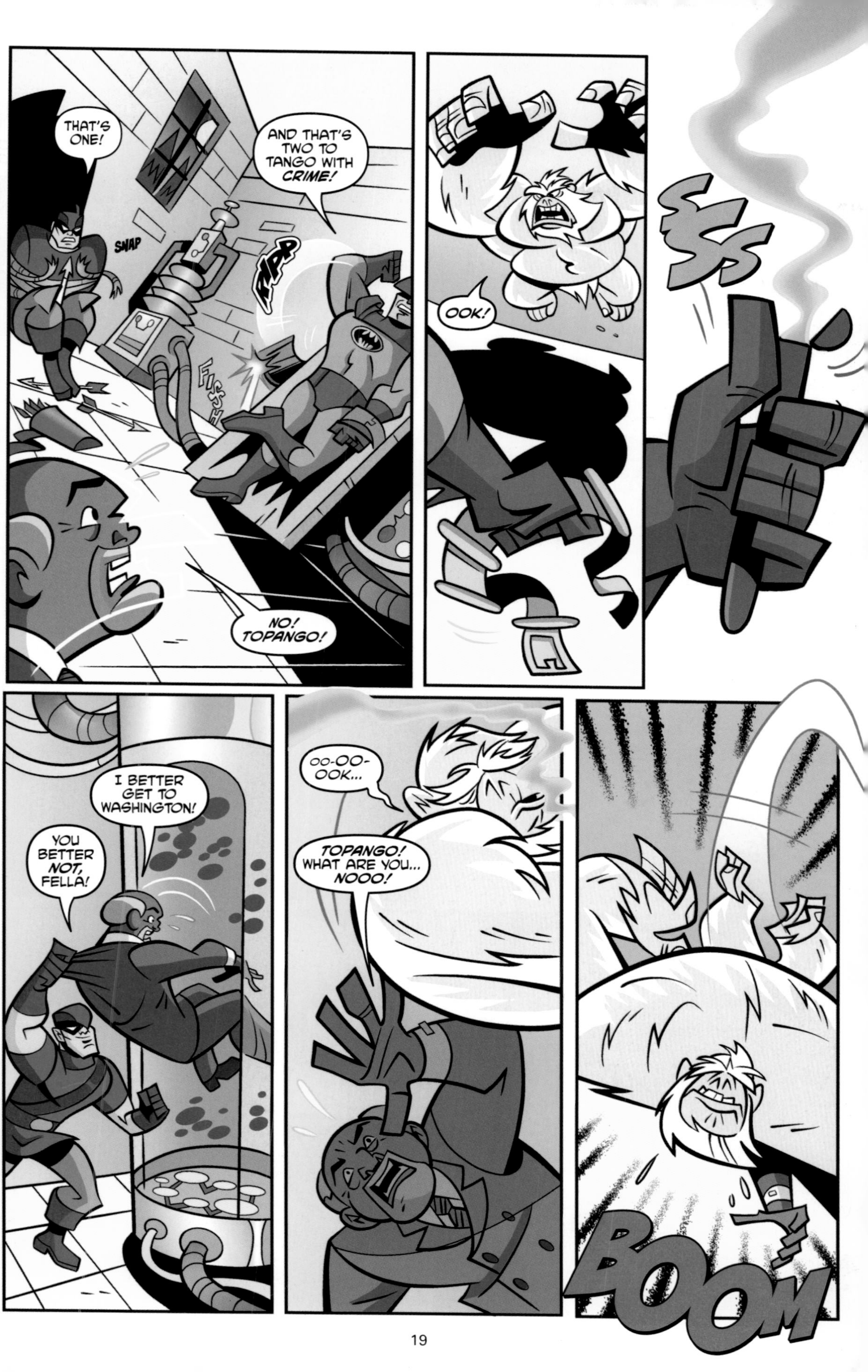
THAT'S ONE!
AND THAT'S TWO TO TANGO WITH CRIME!
SNAP
FISSH
NO! TOPANGO!
OOK!
SSS
I BETTER GET TO WASHINGTON!
YOU BETTER NOT, FELLA!
OO-OO-OOK...
TOPANGO! WHAT ARE YOU... NOOO!
BOOM

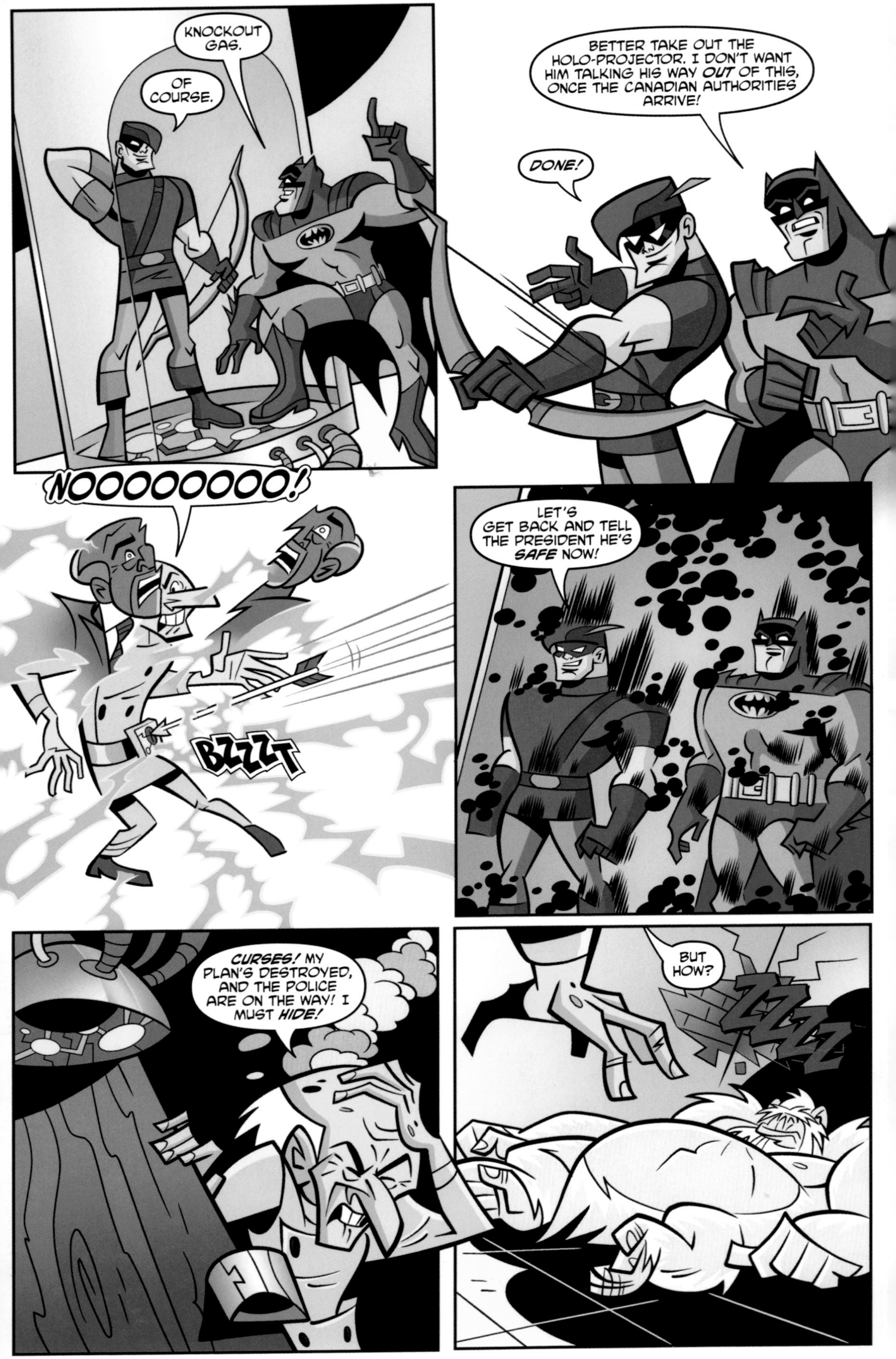
KNOCKOUT GAS.
OF COURSE.
BETTER TAKE OUT THE HOLO-PROJECTOR. I DON'T WANT HIM TALKING HIS WAY OUT OF THIS, ONCE THE CANADIAN AUTHORITIES ARRIVE!
DONE!
NOOOOOOOOO!
BZZZT
LET'S GET BACK AND TELL THE PRESIDENT HE'S SAFE NOW!
CURSES! MY PLAN'S DESTROYED, AND THE POLICE ARE ON THE WAY! I MUST HIDE!
BUT HOW?
ZZZZ

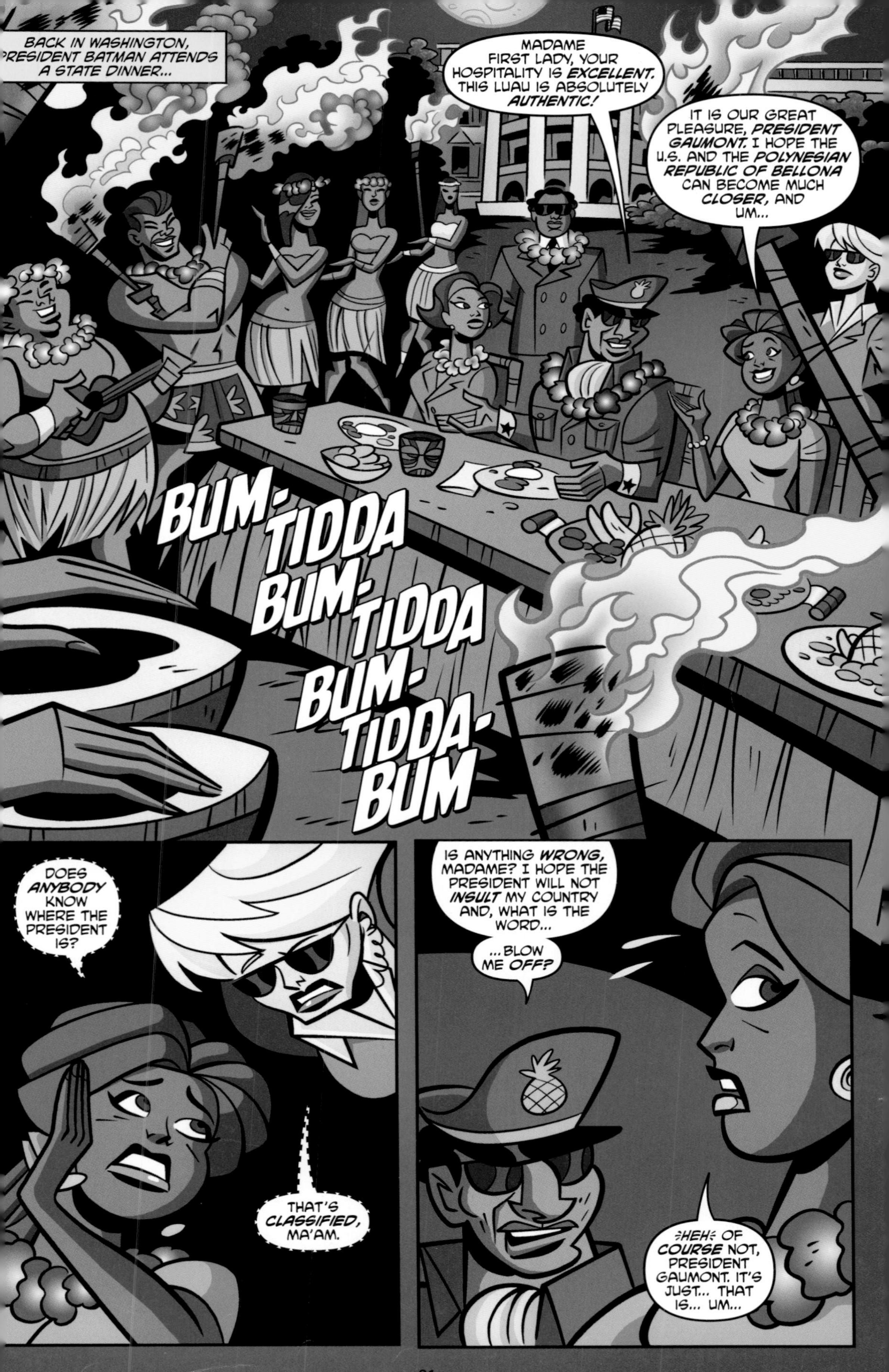
BACK IN WASHINGTON, PRESIDENT BATMAN ATTENDS A STATE DINNER...
MADAME FIRST LADY, YOUR HOSPITALITY IS EXCELLENT. THIS LUAU IS ABSOLUTELY AUTHENTIC!
IT IS OUR GREAT PLEASURE, PRESIDENT GAUMONT. I HOPE THE U.S. AND THE POLYNESIAN REPUBLIC OF BELLONA CAN BECOME MUCH CLOSER, AND UM...
BUM-TIDDA BUM-TIDDA BUM-TIDDA-BUM
DOES ANYBODY KNOW WHERE THE PRESIDENT IS?
THAT'S CLASSIFIED, MA'AM.
IS ANYTHING WRONG, MADAME? I HOPE THE PRESIDENT WILL NOT INSULT MY COUNTRY AND, WHAT IS THE WORD...
...BLOW ME OFF?
HEH OF COURSE NOT, PRESIDENT GAUMONT. IT'S JUST... THAT IS... UM...

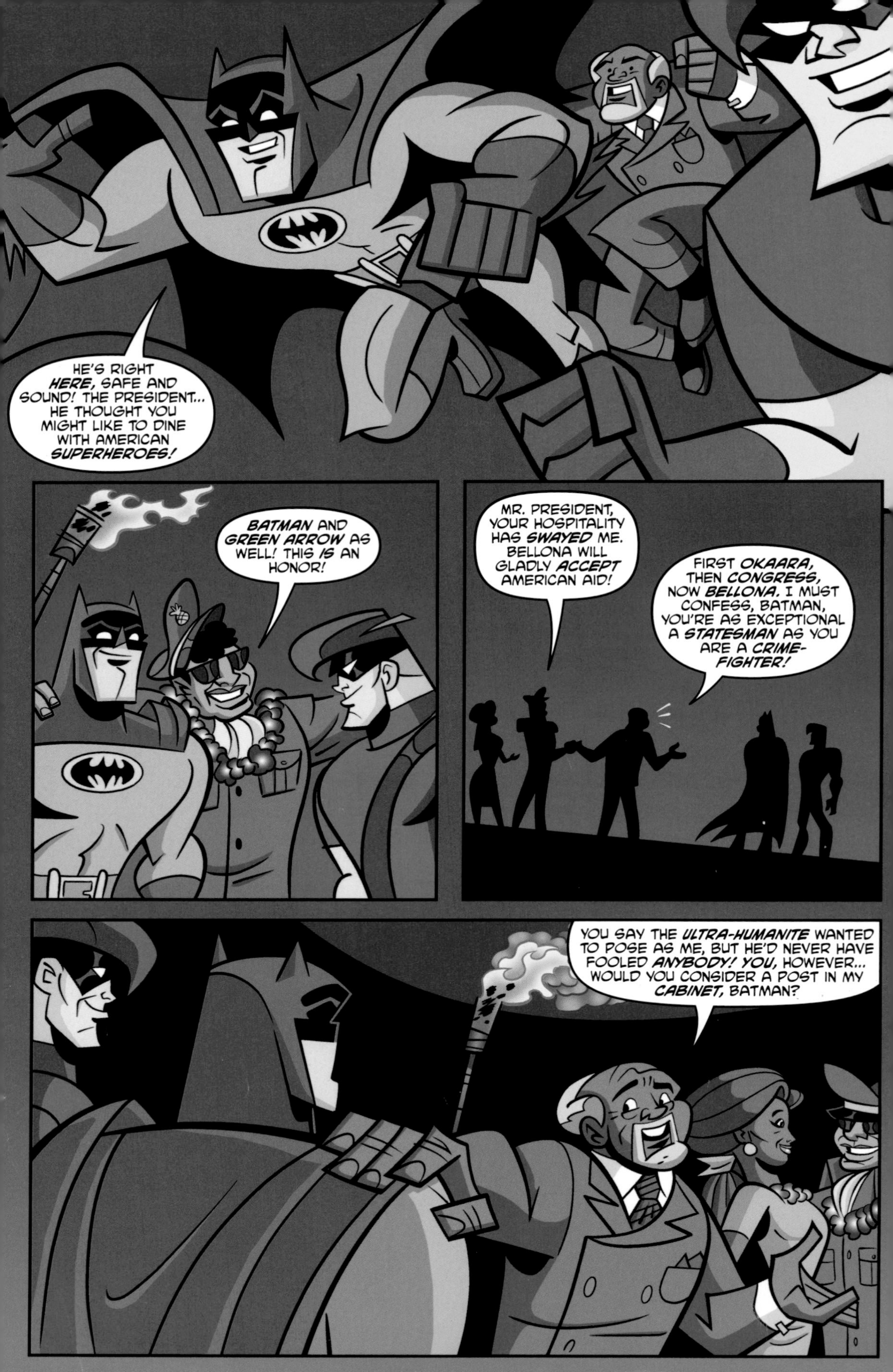
HE'S RIGHT HERE, SAFE AND SOUND! THE PRESIDENT... HE THOUGHT YOU MIGHT LIKE TO DINE WITH AMERICAN SUPERHEROES!
BATMAN AND GREEN ARROW AS WELL! THIS IS AN HONOR!
MR. PRESIDENT, YOUR HOSPITALITY HAS SWAYED ME. BELLONA WILL GLADLY ACCEPT AMERICAN AID!
FIRST OKAARA, THEN CONGRESS, NOW BELLONA. I MUST CONFESS, BATMAN, YOU'RE AS EXCEPTIONAL A STATESMAN AS YOU ARE A CRIME-FIGHTER!
YOU SAY THE ULTRA-HUMANITE WANTED TO POSE AS ME, BUT HE'D NEVER HAVE FOOLED ANYBODY! YOU, HOWEVER... WOULD YOU CONSIDER A POST IN MY CABINET, BATMAN?

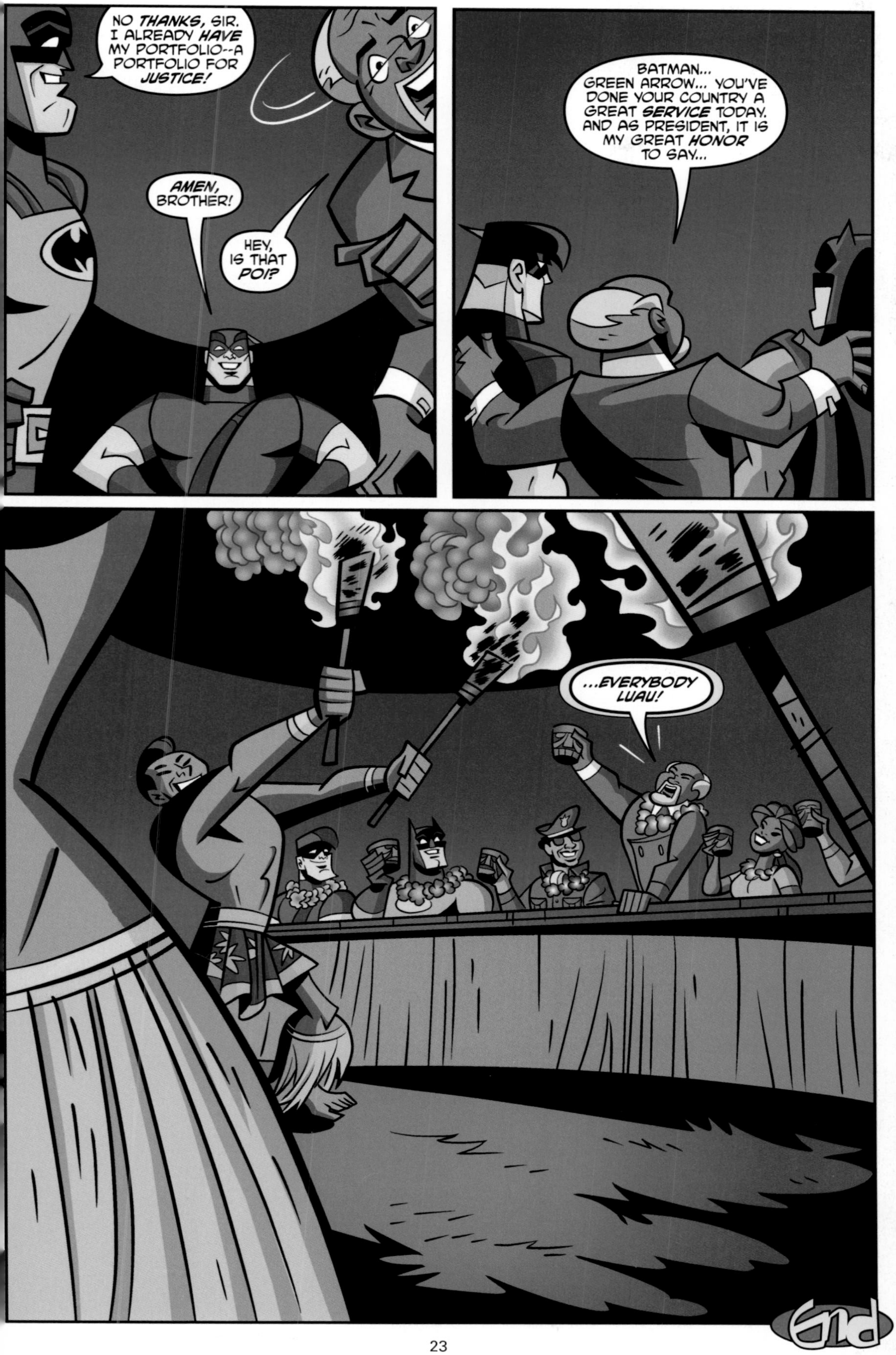
NO *THANKS,* SIR. I ALREADY *HAVE* MY PORTFOLIO--A PORTFOLIO FOR *JUSTICE!*
AMEN, BROTHER!
HEY, IS THAT *POI?*
BATMAN... GREEN ARROW... YOU'VE DONE YOUR COUNTRY A GREAT *SERVICE* TODAY. AND AS PRESIDENT, IT IS MY GREAT *HONOR* TO SAY...
...EVERYBODY LUAU!
End

THE ULTRA-HUMANITE

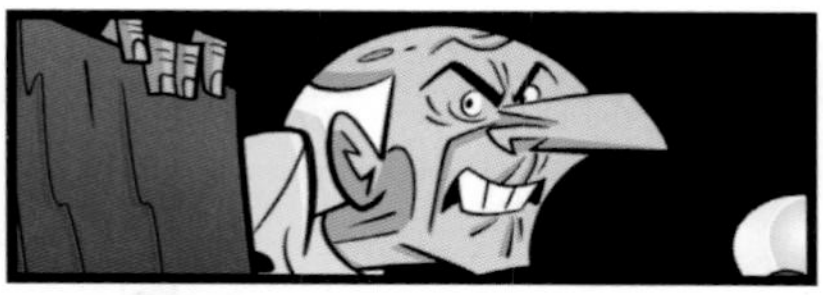

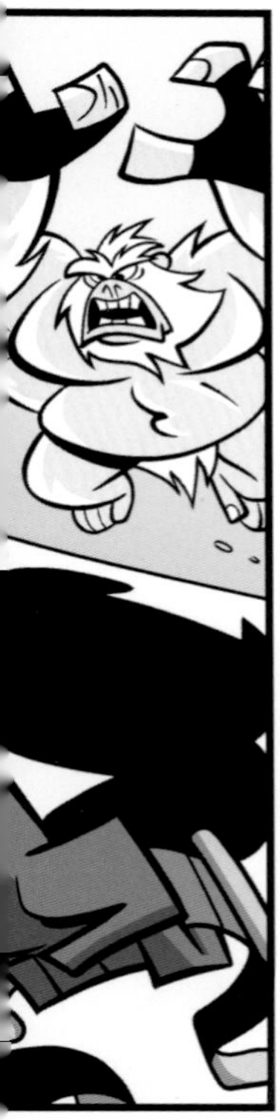

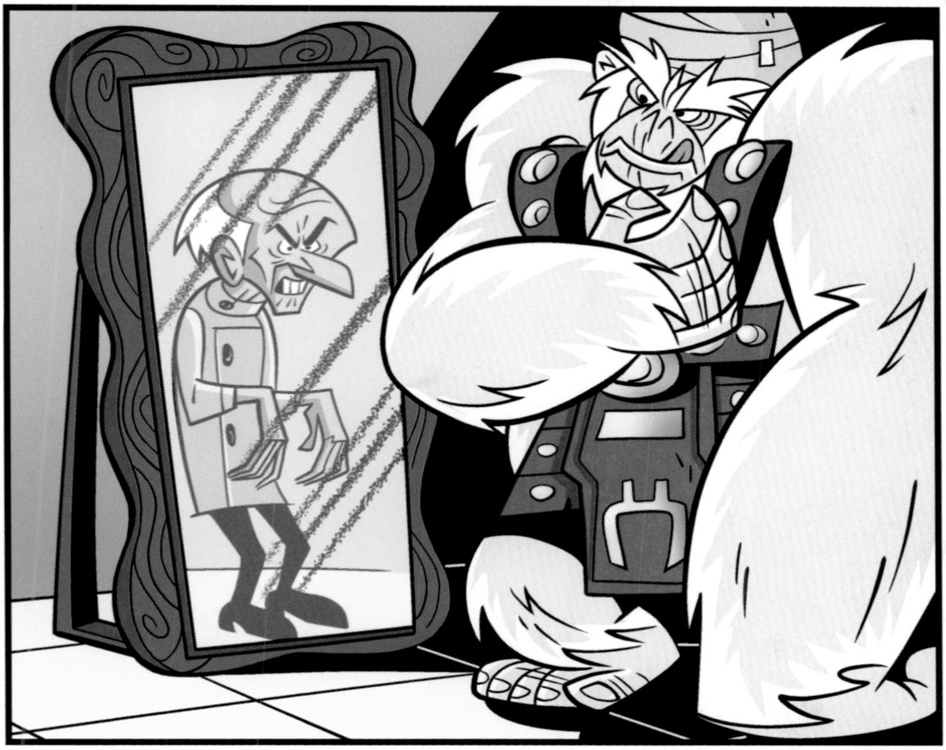

The Ultra-Humanite considers his criminal mind to be the most evolved in the universe. After developing a "hot-swappable" brain case in a failed scheme to take over the United States, the Ultra-Humanite settled for putting his brain into the body of a powerful gorilla.

TOP SECRET:
The real reason the Ultra-Humanite put his brain in a gorilla's body: to stop people from confusing him with the other mad scientist, Luthor.

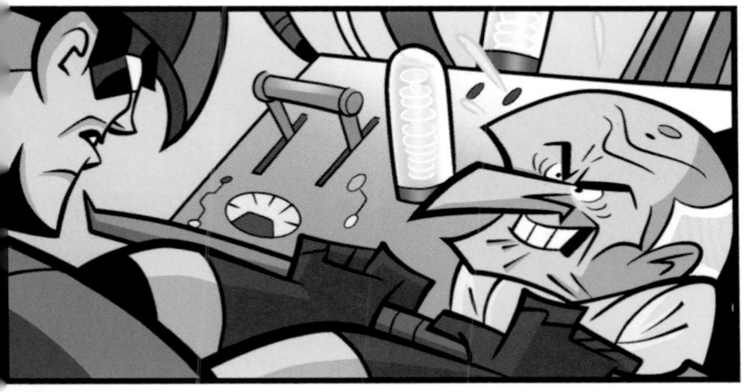

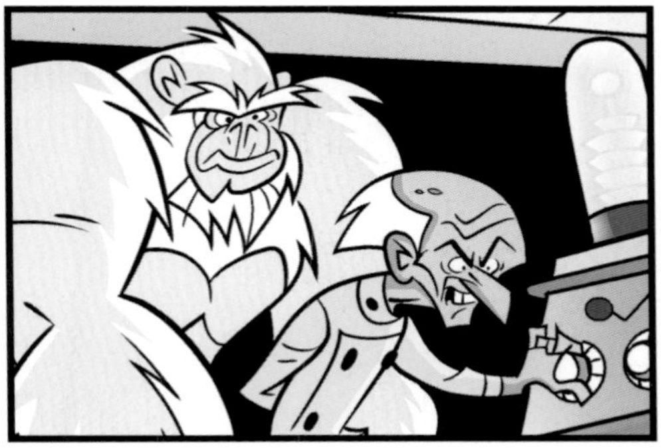

GREEN ARROW

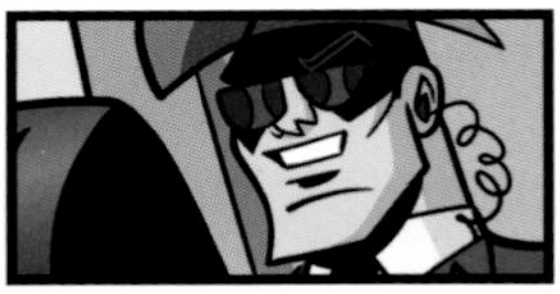

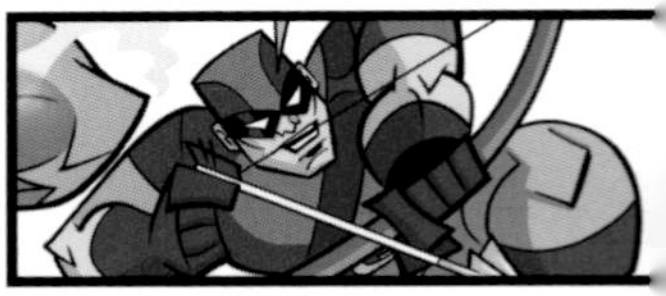

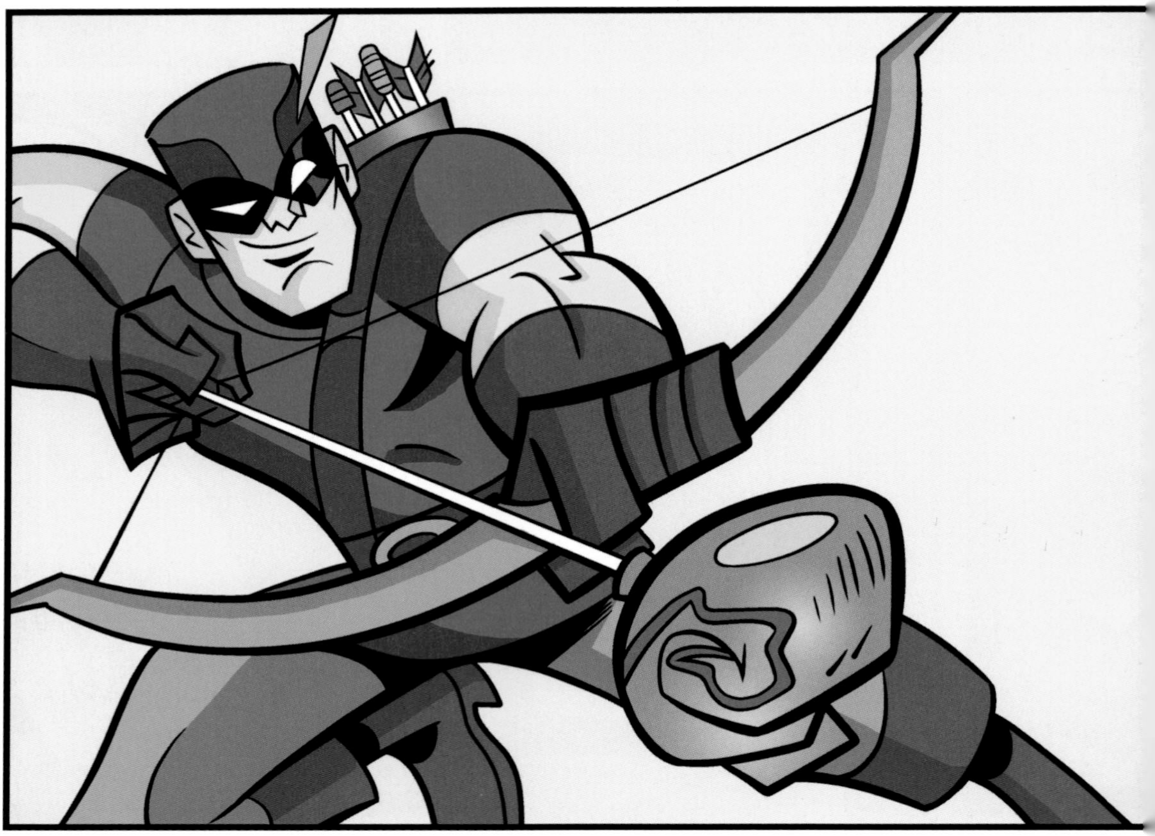

A wealthy businessman turned hero, expert archer Oliver Queen fights crime as straight-shooting Green Arrow. His quiver contains dozens of "trick" arrows. Some cleverly dispense explosives, acid, and sleep gas, while others are more whimsical, such as the infamously effective boxing-glove arrow.

TOP SECRET:
Ollie was fighting crime for months before he realized he'd unconsciously copied Robin Hood's costume.

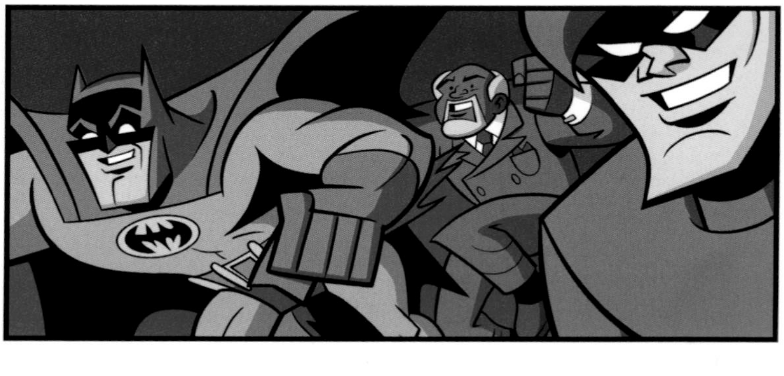

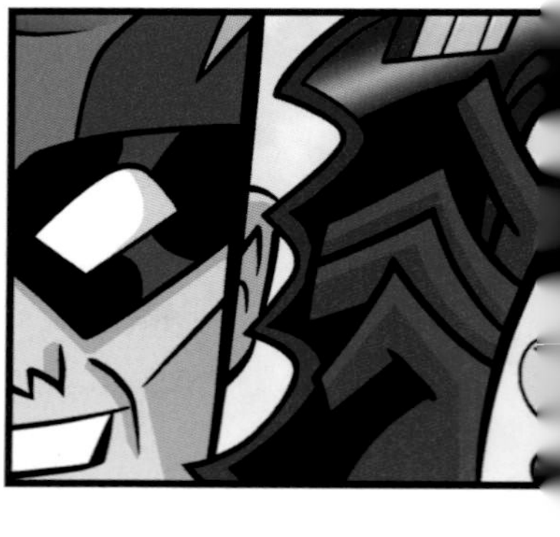

CREATORS

MATT WAYNE WRITER

Matt Wayne is a writer who has worked on TV series including *Ben 10: Ultimate Alien*, *Static Shock*, *Danny Phantom*, and the animated movie *Hellboy: Storm of Swords*. He was an editor at Milestone Media, and has written comics including *Hardware*, *Shadow Cabinet*, *Justice League Unlimited*, and more.

ANDY SURIANO PENCILLER

Andy Suriano is an illustrator of both comic books and animation. His comic book credits include *Batman: The Brave and the Bold* and *Doc Bizarre, M.D.* He's worked on popular animated television series as well, such as *Samurai Jack* and *Star Wars: The Clone Wars*.

DAN DAVIS INKER

Dan Davis is a comic illustrator for DC Comics, Warner Bros., and Bongo. His work has been nominated for several Eisner Awards, including his work on *Batman: The Brave and the Bold*. During his career, Davis has illustrated Batman, The Simpsons, Harry Potter, Samurai Jack, and many other well-known characters!

GLOSSARY

democracy [di·MOK·ruh·see] - a way of governing a country in which the people choose their leader in elections

formidable [FOR·muh·duh·buhl] - frightening, as in a formidable opponent

flummox [FLUH·muhks] - confuse

hypnotize [HIP·nuh·tize] - to put someone into a trance

lunatic [LOO·nuh·tik] - insane or wildly foolish

nefarious [ni·FARE·ee·uhss] - very wicked or evil

ransom [RAN·suhm] - money that is demanded before someone who is being held captive can be set free

ruse [ROOZ] - a clever trick meant to confuse or mislead someone

VISUAL QUESTIONS & PROMPTS

1. Super-villains and other comic book characters often have distinctive features. The illustration below includes four villains: Clock King, Killer Croc, Two-Face, and Scarecrow. Which one is which? Explain how you made your choices, describing each character's physical features.

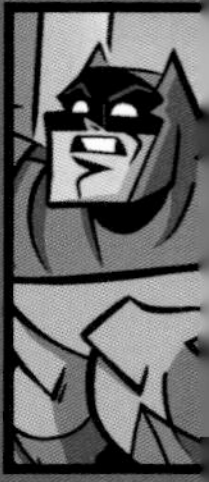

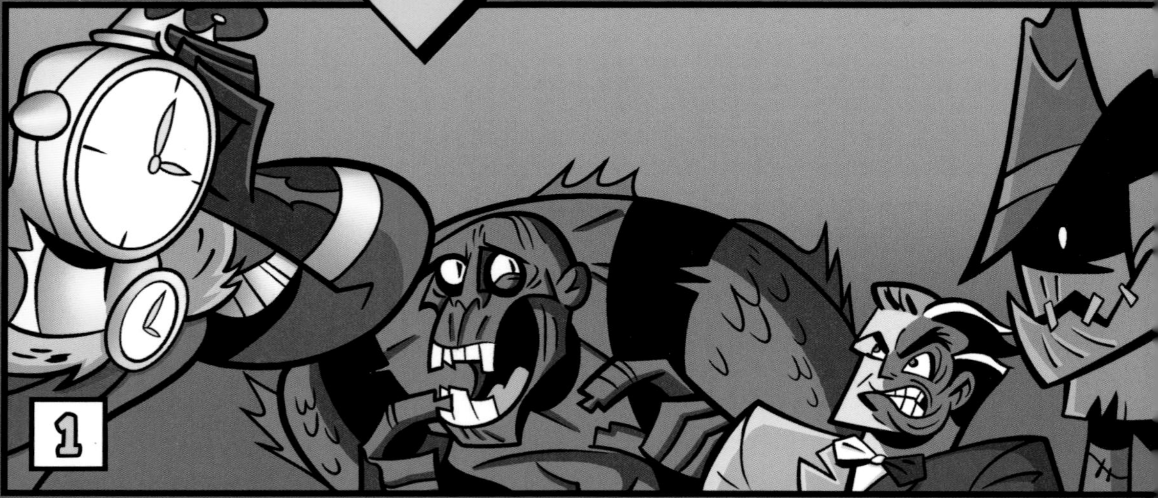
1

2. Describe what is happening in the panel below. Why do you think the creators chose to show only half of Green Arrow and half of Batman? Explain your answer.

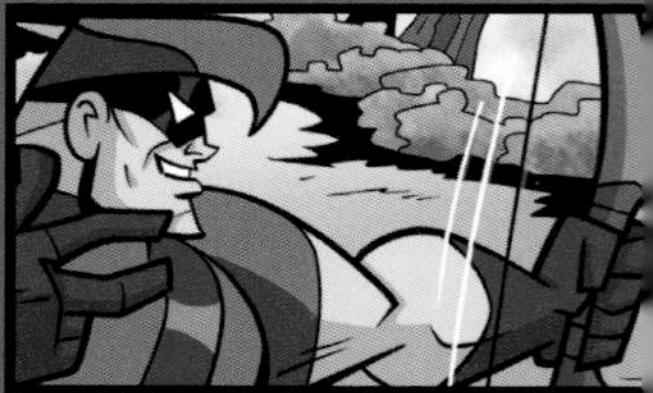

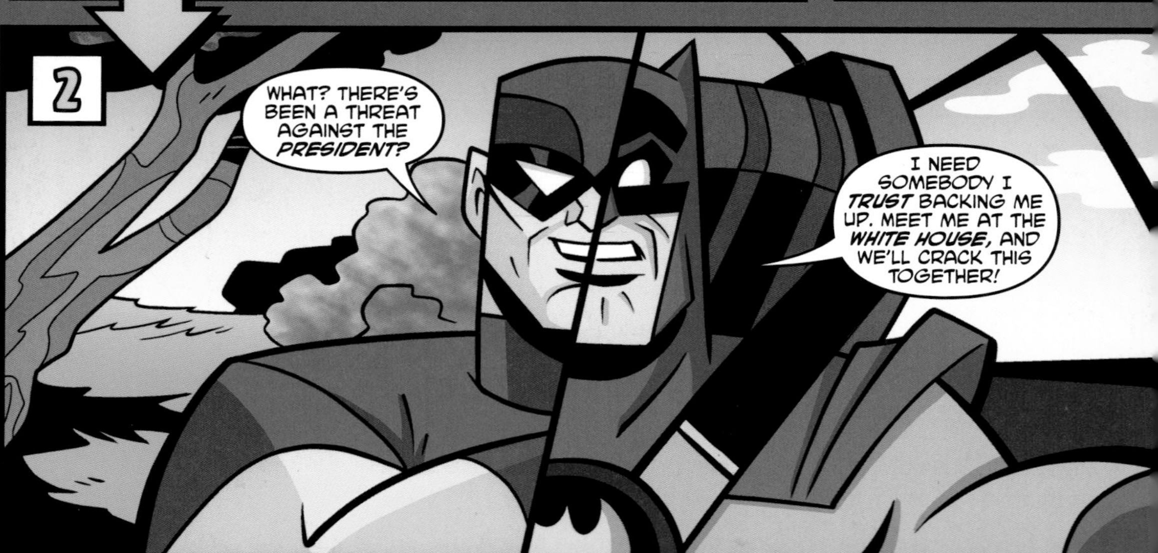
2
WHAT? THERE'S BEEN A THREAT AGAINST THE *PRESIDENT?*
I NEED SOMEBODY I *TRUST* BACKING ME UP. MEET ME AT THE *WHITE HOUSE,* AND WE'LL CRACK THIS TOGETHER!

3. In comic books, the text and illustrations work together to create a complete story. Describe what is happening in the panels below. How did the text and the illustrations help you figure this out?

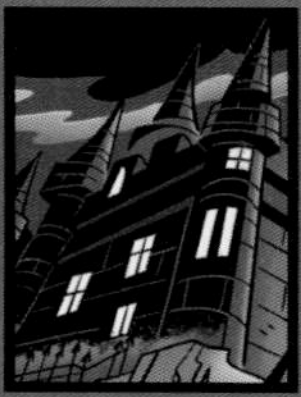

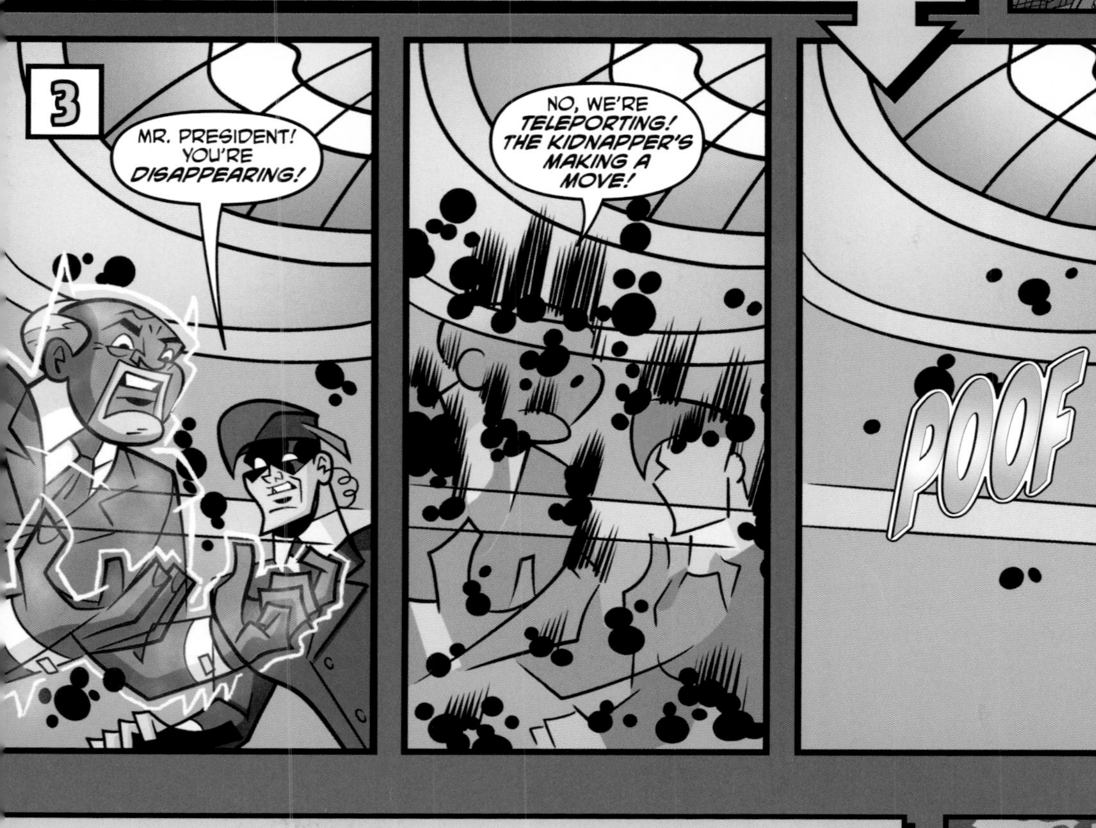
3
MR. PRESIDENT! YOU'RE DISAPPEARING!
NO, WE'RE TELEPORTING! THE KIDNAPPER'S MAKING A MOVE!
POOF

4. In this book, Batman and Green Arrow are both in disguise. Describe how you were able to recognize these two characters, even though they weren't wearing their super hero uniforms.

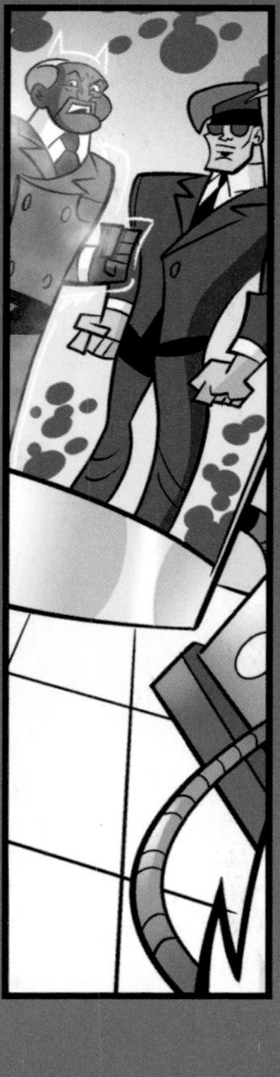

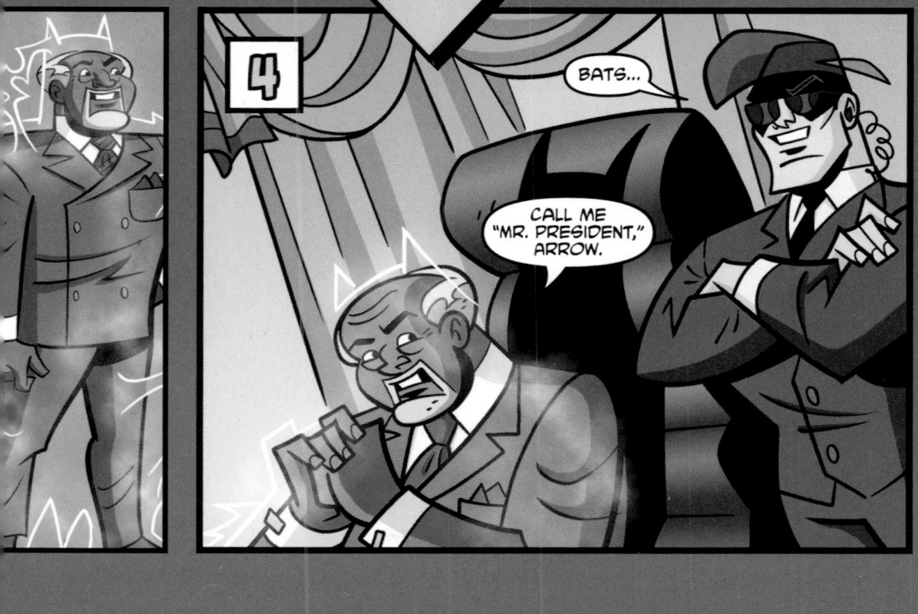
4
BATS...
CALL ME "MR. PRESIDENT," ARROW.

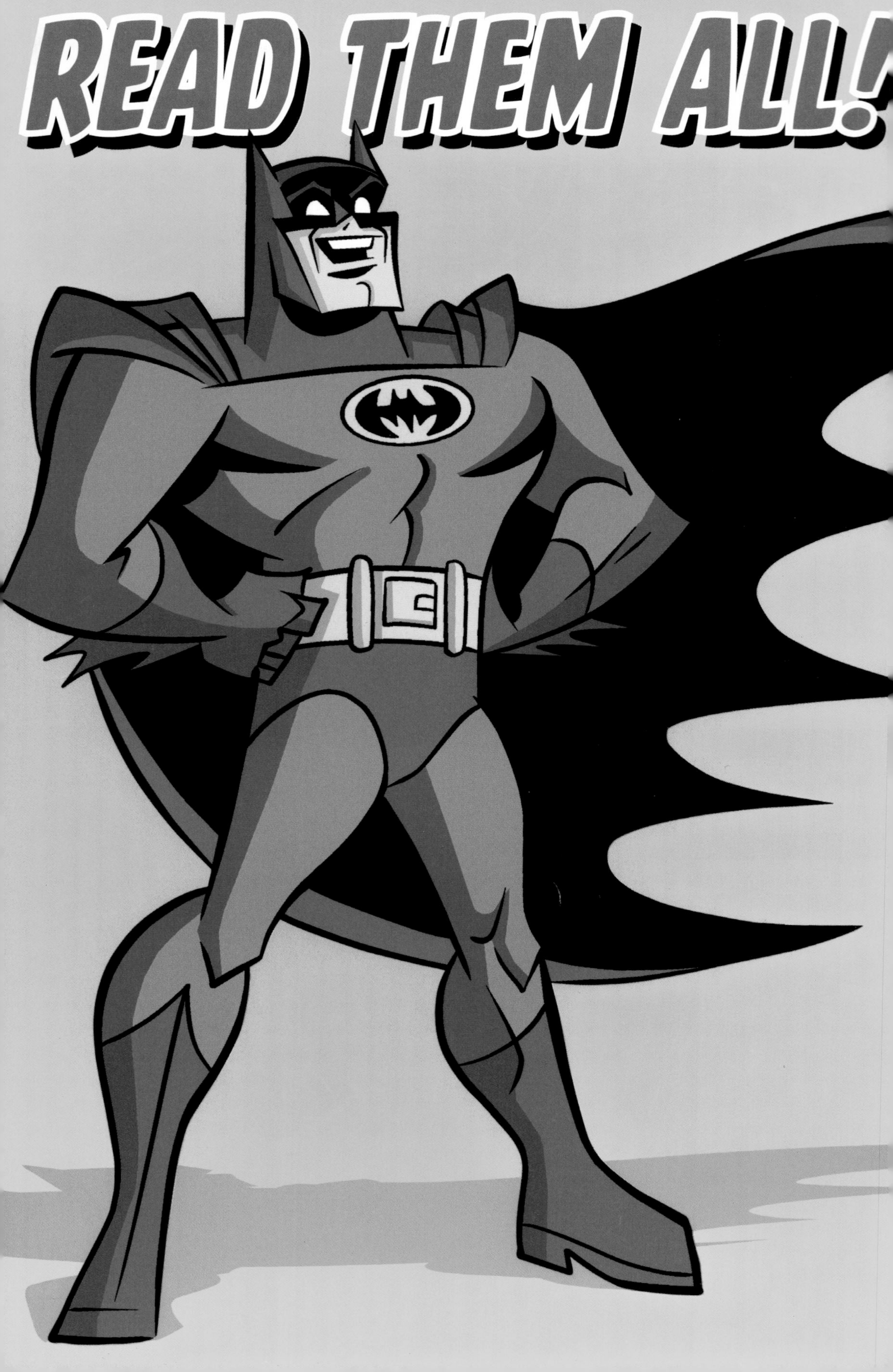
READ THEM ALL!

BATMAN
THE BRAVE AND THE BOLD.

THE PANIC OF THE COMPOSITE CREATURES

THE ATTACK OF THE VIRTUAL VILLAINS

PRESIDENT BATMAN

MENACE OF THE TIME THIEF

ONLY FROM...